never blame
the umpire

We want to hear from you. Please send your comments about this book to us in care of zreview@zondervan.com. Thank you.

ZONDERKIDZ

Never Blame the Umpire
Copyright © 2010 by Gene Fehler

Requests for information should be addressed to:

Zonderkidz, *Grand Rapids, Michigan* 49530

Library of Congress Cataloging-in-Publication Data

Fehler, Gene, 1940
    Never blame the umpire / by Gene Fehler.
  Max Meyers.
     p. cm.
    Summary: Eleven-year-old Kate is having a wonderful summer, playing baseball and taking a poetry class, until her mother is diagnosed with terminal cancer, causing Kate to struggle to keep her faith and trust in God.
    ISBN 978-0-310-71941-0 (hardcover)
    [1. Death—Fiction. 2. Cancer—Fiction. 3. Christian life—Fiction. 4. Family life—Fiction. 5. Poetry—Fiction. 6. Baseball—Fiction.] I. Title.
PZ7.F3318Nev 2010
[fic]—dc22   2009021155

Editor: Kathleen Kerr
Cover design: Cindy Davis
Interior design: Carlos Eluterio Estrada

Printed in the United States of America

10 11 12 13 14 15 /DCI/ 6 5 4 3 2 1

gene fehler

never blame
the umpire

ZONDERVAN.com/
AUTHORTRACKER
follow your favorite authors

This book is dedicated
To all who have lost a loved one—
To my family, as always, with love—
And to my editor, Kathleen Kerr, with gratitude.
G.F.

one

a chance to be a hero

I'm in the on-deck circle, praying for Cal to get a hit. My hands are all sweaty, so I drop my bat on the ground and scoop up a handful of dirt. I rub my hands on my shirt. I don't mind getting dirty. Mama and Dad don't care how dirty I get, either. They just say, "It's part of the game, Kate. If you're really playing hard, you're bound to get dirty. But you already know that."

I do. I've played enough sports with Mama and Dad and my little brother Ken to know it. This is my first summer of playing baseball on a real team. We've been practicing for a couple of weeks, but this is our first game. This is my first time playing base-ball under pressure.

I pick up my bat and study the pitcher. Coach always tells us to watch the pitcher closely, especially when we're on deck, so we can get an idea how hard he's throwing.

If Cal doesn't end the game right now with a hit, I might have a chance to win the game and be a hero. The trouble is, I'm not a great hitter. I have an even better chance of making the final out. I sure don't want to do that.

I take my eyes off the pitcher long enough to glance back toward the bleachers. Mama and Dad still aren't here. The last thing they'd said before they left home this morning was, "We wouldn't miss your game for anything."

Why aren't they here?

They were supposed to be home before 5:30, which is when Ken and I had to be at the field. We were all going to go together. They didn't come home, and they didn't even call. So Ken and I had to go without them. Luckily, our ballfield is only four blocks from our house. Ken and I ran all the way here and got here just in time.

Now it's the bottom of the sixth. We're one run behind. Ken led off the inning with a single. He's only ten, a whole year younger than me, but he's a better hitter. After Ken singled, Jack popped out and Andy doubled. Their left fielder made a nice play to keep Ken from scoring the tying run. Now, with just one out, a fly ball or maybe even a ground ball could tie the game. The bad thing is, Cal doesn't hit any better than I do.

Even though I'm not one of the best players, I really wanted for Mama and Dad to see me play my first game. Even though Ken has played ever since t-ball, I was never that into it. Ivy Snow talked me into playing. Next to Ginny, she's my best friend. She played last year, and she was the only girl on the team. This year we have three girls on the team: Ivy, Heather, and me. We tried to get Ginny to play, but we couldn't talk her into it.

The pitch comes in, a foot over Cal's head. He swings. He couldn't have reached it unless he were standing on a ladder.

"Come on, Cal!" I shout. "Make the pitch be in there!"

What I'm thinking is, "Please, please get that run in!"

I really, really don't want to make the last out with the tying run on third.

The next pitch is in the strike zone, and Cal hits a dinky infield pop-up. The second baseman doesn't even have to move. He catches it with two hands and flips the ball back to the pitcher.

Now it's up to me. The only good thing about Mama and Dad not being here is that they won't have to see me make the last out. It's not like them to not keep their word. Maybe they had a flat tire or something. I can't think of a good reason why they're not here. Some of my friends complain that their parents always break promises. But I've never had that problem. Mama and Dad have a lot of pet sayings, and one of them is, "Never make a promise unless you plan to keep it."

I try to focus on the pitcher. All that matters right now is, can I hit the ball? I hold my bat in one hand and jerk at the bill of my green cap with my other hand. In my first at-bat my cap wasn't on tight enough. It flew off my head when I swung hard and missed, striking out. I heard some people laugh. I wasn't sure if they laughed because my cap flew off and I looked silly or because I missed the ball. My second time up I at least hit the ball, but it was just a weak grounder back to the pitcher.

I hope nobody can see how bad I'm shaking. I didn't expect to be this nervous. I've played a lot of tennis with my mom and dad and brother. Mama played tennis on her college team, and she taught Ken and me. We're pretty good. We've had plenty of tight matches where I've had to return serve at match point, but I've never been as scared as I am now. I guess that's because I'm better at hitting a tennis ball than I am at hitting a baseball.

Maybe I'll get lucky and the pitcher will walk me. I hope. Making the last out would be a perfectly awful way to start the season.

I tap home plate with the fat end of the red aluminum bat. The pitcher looks in at me, or maybe at his catcher. Toby shouts to me from the on-deck circle. I suddenly realize I don't really want to walk. I know I have a better chance to get a hit than Toby does. He's struck out both times, not once coming close to making contact with the ball. Even in batting practice, he hardly ever hits the ball. If our team, the Colby Panthers, is going to win our opening game of the season, I'm afraid it's up to me.

"Bring me home, Kate!" Ken shouts from third base. "You can do it!"

I hear Coach call out, "Okay, Kate. Wait for your pitch."

I don't hear the voices I want to hear the most: Mama's and Dad's.

I grip the bat as tight as I can to try to stop my hands from shaking. I stare at the ball in the pitcher's hand. His hand starts to move and now the ball is coming toward me. I want to swing, but my arms don't move.

"Ball!" the ump calls out.

"Way to look!" Ken yells. "Make him throw strikes!"

He doesn't know that the only reason I didn't swing was because I'm too scared.

"No hitter no hitter no hitter," their catcher

chatters. Unfortunately, he's right.

The second pitch comes in waist high, right over the heart of the plate. The pitcher couldn't have thrown me an easier pitch to hit if he'd tried all day. My mind shouts, "Swing! Swing!" but my arms stay frozen again. The ump yells, "Strike one!"

I pound my bat hard on home plate, just to prove that my arms really do move. Small clouds of dust puff up.

I've gone out twice, but at least I hit the ball once. Why won't my arms work now?

And they do, finally. But the pitch comes in low, at my ankles. I swing over the top of it. One more strike and we've lost the game.

Their catcher's thinking the same thing because he calls out, "One more strike. No hitter no hitter. Just throw it in here."

I take a deep breath. I look hard at the pitcher. He looks nervous too ... at least I tell myself he does. It makes me feel a little bit better. I try not to watch him, though. I try to focus on the ball. He holds it in his right hand. Then the ball disappears in his glove and his arms go above his head. His right arm comes down, pointing right toward me, and now I see the ball again. I hold back a split second longer on this pitch than I did on the other one. When I see it's going to be close to the outside corner, I swing.

I'm surprised at how loud the sound is when

my bat meets the ball. I watch the ball take off on a line toward right field, and I start to run. It lands in front of the right fielder. I see him field it cleanly and throw it toward home. I turn and watch the ball bounce twice before the catcher fields it. He catches the ball just as Andy slides into him. The two players are covered by a cloud of dust.

The ump stands over them with his arms spread in the "safe" signal. Andy scrambles to his feet and starts to whoop. He tosses his cap into the air.

The whole team races out toward me, Ken leading the pack. I'm jumping up and down. I can't help it. I just never thought I would get a hit.

I feel really great. But I can't stop myself from glancing again at the bleachers. I can't stop myself from wishing that Mama and Dad were here to see it.

two

post-game

Coach breaks up our celebration so our team can walk single-file across the middle of the infield to shake hands with the players from the other team. It's a league rule. Be good sports, whether you win or lose. That's what Coach preaches to us at every practice. "Play hard," he says, "but most of all play fair and have fun." He always tells us, "We should all play to win, because that's what makes competition fun, but I'd much rather coach a team of good losers than a team of poor winners."

I'm really glad he's coaching us. Ken and I have known him for a long time. He teaches Sunday

School at my church and comes along with our youth
group on a lot of our activities. The best thing about
having him as a coach is he doesn't yell and get
mad like some of the other coaches do. If we make
a mistake, like throwing the ball to the wrong base
or something, he'll talk to us and tell us the right
thing to do. And he always does it in a quiet way. He
never shouts or makes anybody feel bad like some
of the other coaches do. Ken played last year, and I
went to almost all his games. I couldn't believe how
mean some of the other coaches were to their players.
In one game the shortstop on the other team made
an error and his coach came right out on the field
and yelled at him to go to the bench and he brought
another kid in to take his place. Right in the middle
of the inning!

Coach motions for all of us to get together down
the left field line. It's our "post-game critique." He
says we'll be having one after every game because it's
important to go over things that happen in the game
while they're still fresh in everybody's mind.

The things that are really fresh in my mind are
that last swing, the sound the bat made when the
ball hit it, and Ken and Andy scoring the tying and
winning runs.

"Remember that base hit they got back in the
fourth inning?" Coach says. "The one out to right-
center that Heather fielded? When the runner on first

base was running toward third, the pitcher should have been backing up the base in case the throw got away. That goes for everybody. Always anticipate where the ball will be thrown and back up the base."

I can hardly wait for Coach to get to the good part, that last inning.

"Another thing," Coach says. "Pay attention to my signs. Twice I gave the bunt sign and the batter swung anyway. Missing a sign is serious business. It can cost a team a game. I remember a game two years ago when a player missed the bunt sign and then grounded into a double play to end the game." Coach has such a serious look on his face you'd think we lost the game.

Suddenly his face breaks into a big smile. "Enough of the negatives," he says. "I'm proud of all of you. You played hard, and you never gave up."

Coach takes a couple minutes to tell at least one good thing everybody did in the game, even Cal, who struck out twice and popped out and missed the only two balls hit to him. Coach said, "Cal, you did a great job battling up there at the plate that last inning. Keep it up and the hits will start dropping."

I can hardly wait until he gets to me.

"Ken, Andy, you two set the table for Kate in that last inning with good hits. And Kate, what a clutch hit that was. Two strikes and you hung in there. That was a fine piece of hitting."

Everybody starts to cheer.

Coach shouts out above the cheers, "No practice or game tomorrow. We'll practice Saturday morning at ten. See you then. Remember, if you know ahead of time you can't make it, be sure to call me and let me know."

Some of our players leave with their parents. Some others get on their bikes. I call out to Ken, "Race you home!"

"You're on!" Ken answers.

Ken's the better baseball player, but I'm the faster runner. Besides, I already have a three or four step head start. I know there's no way he can catch me.

I fling open our screen door and burst through first. Dad's standing by the window.

"We won!" I shout. "We won!"

Ken blurts, "Kate got the hit that drove me and Andy in with the tying and winning runs."

"It was the last of . . ." I begin. But I stop when Dad turns toward me. His eyes are red and puffy.

"Hi kids," he says. His voice is soft, almost a whisper. "Sorry we missed your game. How'd you do?"

We've already told him. Didn't he even hear us? I glance at Ken. He's looking at me with a puzzled look on his face.

"We won," I said. "6 to 5."

Dad doesn't say anything. He just nods.

"Is anything wrong?" I ask. I realize Mama's not

in the room. "Is Mama okay?"

"Your mom's not feeling well. She went to bed early."

I glance at the wall clock. 8:10. Mama, in bed? She's never in bed by 8:10. Never. Unless she has the flu or something. And she's almost never sick.

"She's not asleep yet, is she?" I ask. "Maybe she'd like to hear about the game."

"I think we'd better let her rest," Dad said. "You can tell her about the game tomorrow."

"She's not real sick, is she?" Ken says. "She was all right this morning."

Dad doesn't look at us. He just stands by the window, looking into the backyard. "I'm sorry we didn't get home in time for your game. There's some macaroni in the fridge that you can microwave. I'm going to go check on your mother."

He turns and heads toward the bedroom. Before he gets there, I say, "Dad?"

He stops and turns his head.

"Can I just see if Mama's awake and say goodnight?"

Dad smiles. Or at least tries to. It's not his normal smile.

"It's best to let her rest. You can tell her about the game tomorrow," he says. "She'll be fine."

But the way he says it doesn't sound at all convincing.

three

ginny

Ken and I are sitting in front of the TV eating our microwaved dinner when my cell phone rings.

"Did you win your game?" Ginny asks.

"You should have been there!" Of course I know better than anybody that Ginny and baseball don't mix. After all, she's been my best friend for years. We've always been in the same classes at school, and we even go to the same church. We've been in the same Sunday School classes and youth groups. We do almost everything together.

Except baseball. Even Coach has tried to talk her into playing, but she won't. I'm going to keep working on her. Ivy and Heather said they'll keep trying, too. Baseball would be even more fun if Ginny was on the team.

I tell her about that last inning. Everything. How scared I was and then how I felt when I hit the ball and it fell in for a base hit.

"That would have been fun to see," she says. "Kate Adams, Girl Heroine. Maybe I'll even come to one of your games sometime."

"Do you mean it? Ginny Calhoun, at a baseball game?"

"Sure, I don't mind watching."

"Hey, maybe there's hope for you after all."

Ginny giggles. "I wouldn't go that far. When it comes to baseball, I'm hopeless. I'll come only if you promise to be the heroine again."

"Oh, sure. No problem. I'll probably get the game-winning hit every time."

"You'd better. I'm counting on it."

I take a bite of my microwaved macaroni and cheese and let my thoughts drift back to that moment when I saw the umpire signal "safe."

"I bet your mother totally flipped out," Ginny says. "The last time I talked to her she was really excited about you and Ken playing your first game together. I remember how pumped she got during your soccer games last fall. She was the loudest screamer in the crowd."

"She gets excited all right. But she couldn't come to the game today. She's sick."

"That's too bad." I know Ginny means it. That's

one of the things I like best about her: she cares
about people. It's like she actually feels their pain
whenever someone around her is hurting. "Tell her I
hope she's feeling better."

"I will."

"Did you write your poem yet?" Ginny asks.

"Not yet. How about your monologue? Do you
have it memorized?"

"Not quite. It's a long one. I wish you were in
drama. Then we could work together."

"You know I'm no actress," I tell her. "But I wish
you were in creative writing."

She laughs. "You know I'm no poet."

Today was the fourth day of the first week of our
three-week session of classes at the Valley Lake School
for the Arts. Every June our county has fine arts classes
for grades five through eight. Ginny went last year in
drama. She's a really good actress and has been in lots of
plays in our town's children's theater. She always tells me
I should audition. No way. Like I told Ginny, I'm no actress. I've helped her rehearse by reading lines with her. I
just can't read them like a real actress does. Not like she
does. She actually becomes the character. Me, I'm just
reading words. No matter how hard I try, I never get any
better. She must know that, but she's too nice to tell me.

The school has classes in visual arts, music,
dance, drama, and creative writing. The classes
meet from nine o'clock until three o'clock five days a

week. Kids who want to attend have to audition and be selected by the school's faculty.

Last summer was awful because I didn't get to see Ginny much for those three weeks. I didn't audition for anything last year because I wasn't any good in any of the arts or even interested in them.

But this spring a visiting poet came to our school for one week and taught us about writing poetry. I never knew before how much fun it could be to write poems. He read a lot of his own, and they were easy to understand. Most of them were funny. He read a lot of good poems about sports, too. I liked those the best.

He had us write poems ourselves. I didn't think I'd be able to, but he showed us lots of ways to get started. He said that getting those first few words on the page is the most important thing. He had us do some activities that made it really easy to write those first words. Like "begin with a place or a time or a person or action or object. Then combine them." And "think of a person and put the person in a certain place. Have the person doing something." Things like that. Another one was, "Take an object, something you can actually touch. Have someone do something with that object. Add a time and place." And he said a poem doesn't have to rhyme. That made it easier.

He said, "Once you get your poem started, ask 'What next?' or 'What else?' Before you know it, you have a poem." I found out that writing a poem isn't as hard as I thought it would be. Actually, it's kind of fun.

So this summer I auditioned for creative writing. And got chosen!

In my audition, I had to submit a poem I'd written and then have an interview with the teacher. I guess that was how he determined who really deserved to be in his class. At least he could find out who wanted to be there.

I submitted a poem I wrote about soccer.

Soccer Goalie

In the closing seconds
I crouch on coiled legs,
wait for the corner kick.
I spring like a leopard,
claw autumn's misty air,
clutch the damp ball,
clench it in cold hands,
skip three steps on soggy ground,
swing my leg into the ball's flight
and take a tasty bite
of victory's sweet fruit.

In my interview, Mr. Gallagher, the teacher, really surprised me. He said my poem was "marvelous." He was really impressed with my strong verbs. He said, "You captured the moment vividly." Then he asked me about what he called "the process" of writing the poem. I told him about the poet who came to our school and told us we could start with a moment when something happened and then just add details to show what happened during that moment.

Mr. Gallagher said, "Well, you did great. I'm impressed."

So I guess it was that poem that helped me get in his creative writing class. Even though Ginny and I aren't in the same classes, we still see each other a lot. We ride the bus and have lunch together. There's an activity period where we go outside and play volleyball or kickball. And every morning there's an assembly. A guest artist comes to the school and gives a program or lecture. Ginny and I always sit together.

So even though Ginny isn't playing baseball, this summer is better than last summer was.

I tell Ginny, "If I'm going to convince Mr. Gallagher that he was right to choose me, I'd better finish my assignment for tomorrow. I still have one poem to write."

"Okay," Ginny says. "And congratulations on your game-winning hit."

"Thanks. I'll meet you at the bus stop in the morning."

I go back to the living room, pick up my cold

dinner, reheat it in the microwave, and take it to my bedroom. I set it on my desk, open my notebook, pick up a pen, and look at the poem's first line, which I've already written in my notebook:

What I remember most

In class today, Mr. Gallagher had us write that line. One of our assignments for tomorrow is to write an unrhymed poem at least eight lines long using that as our first line. He told us, "Think of a single event in your life. It can be something that happened at any time in your past—five years ago, last year, last month, just a few days ago, or even today. You can make up details if you want, but you can also describe the moment exactly as it occurred. It doesn't have to be a big, dramatic event. You can just start writing about the first thing that pops into your mind."

I know I can do this assignment because it's a lot like what I did with my soccer poem. Just write about a single moment. So I do what he said. I start writing about the first thing that pops into my head, and the lines start to flow. I don't even have to think about what to write. My pen seems to move under its own power as it rushes across my paper. I write the final line and read over what I've written. I realize that I didn't even worry about the length, and the poem turned out to be even longer than Mr. Gallagher said it had to be.

never blame the umpire

What I remember most
 is the way my arms felt
when ball hit bat,
 the way the ball darted,
like a scared rabbit
 toward the outfield,
the way the dust
 billowed above home plate,
the way Andy pumped
 his arm in the air,
the way the team cheered me
and called me a hero,
and the fact that Mama and Dad
weren't there to see any of it.

four

breakfast with mama

I don't know if it's the tapping on the door or Mama's words, but something wakes me from a really good dream—the kind that makes you feel warm inside. I try to hold on to it as long as I can. After the second or third "Kate" I know it's no use. I'll never get back to that wonderful dream.

In the few seconds it takes me to answer Mama's "Time to get up" with "Okay, Mama," I can't even remember what the dream had been about. It was probably something that would have made a good poem or story, but it's gone now.

I wonder if that happens to other people, getting pleasant dreams interrupted right in the best parts and not being able to finish them. Ginny claims she doesn't dream much, but I can't believe that. How can someone not dream? It seems like almost every night I have one dream right after another all night long. When I don't dream, I wake up in the morning feeling a little bit disappointed. To me, the best thing about sleeping isn't even the rest I get, it's the dreams. It's like watching a movie or even reading a story, but without doing the work it takes to actually read a story.

I just wish scientists could find a way to videotape dreams so we could have a permanent record of them. I keep my notebook right next to my bed, and once in awhile I'll grab my pen the second I wake up and scribble out some words or details of the dream so I'll be able to remember it longer. I'm not very good at doing it, though. The details of my dreams always fade after a few seconds. I usually end up with a couple of words or sentences that really don't make much sense when I read them a day or two later. Sometimes I can't even read my scribbling.

A dream is a lot like eating orange sherbet; it's sweet and pleasant and you want the taste to last and last, but it's gone too soon. Nothing is left except the memory that once upon a time something really tasty had been there.

I slip into my summer school clothes—loose fitting denim shorts and a white t-shirt, sneakers, and white socks. The temperature is supposed to be in the low nineties. The director of our school told

us we could dress comfortably, as long as we dress
tastefully. By "tastefully" she means don't show too
much skin and don't wear clothing too tight or with
dirty words written on it. Even if I wanted to dress
that way, which I don't, Mama and Dad would never
permit it, so the school's dress code really isn't a
problem for me.

Mama is standing at the kitchen counter. My
breakfast is waiting for me—a bowl of cold cereal
with a sliced banana, orange juice, and a glass of
milk. I pour half the milk into my bowl of cereal.
Soggy cereal is really gross, so whenever Mama has
breakfast waiting for me, she makes it a point to let
me pour the milk into the bowl myself.

"Hi, Mama. Are you feeling better?"

She smiles. "I am, honey. Thanks." Her eyes
have hints of red in them. She looks tired.

"Are you going in to work today? You look like
you could use some more sleep."

She pours herself a cup of coffee and sits at the
table. "I look that bad?" She says it in a teasing way,
and I can't help but smile.

"You never look bad, you know that. You do look
tired, though."

"I guess I didn't sleep well," she says. She butters
some toast, but doesn't eat it. She just stares at it for
a moment. "I'll be going to work, same as always, as
soon as the bus picks you up. Mr. Randolph's office

would fall apart without me there. You know how it is. Ken's the only one lucky enough to sleep late, now that you have to get up early for your class."

She motions toward the toast. "You want some?"

I shake my head. "Has Dad left already?"

"About twenty minutes ago."

I glance at my watch. I still have plenty of time before I have to walk to the bus stop. "I think you should make Ken get up, too," I say. "I bet there are plenty of chores for him to do while we're all out working so hard."

"Oh, are they working you hard?" There's a twinkle in her eyes. She doesn't seem to be sick. I'm so glad. I was worried about her. I don't remember her ever being too sick to say good-night to me. Until last night.

"In last night's game I could hardly hold the bat, my hand was so stiff from all the writing that Mr. Gallagher has us do."

"Your hand must not have hurt too badly. Your father told me that you got the game-winning hit. I wish I could have seen it. I'm so proud of you. I can imagine how exciting it must have been."

"Oh, it was! Remember, you told us about the time you won the conference tennis championship in a tie-breaker that lasted forever. And how exciting that was. 15–13, wasn't it? But I bet I was even more excited about my hit than you were about winning that championship."

Mama smiles. Then she gets this faraway look in her eyes. It's like she's looking past me, maybe back to that tennis match. She blinks hard a couple of times, then looks back at me. "I'm glad," she says.

"Who knows, maybe I'll have another chance. It's a long season. Thirteen more games. I was talking to Ginny last night and she said she might even start coming to some of them."

Mama gets up from the table and carries her plate to the dishwasher. "That would be nice. She's not much of a baseball fan, is she?"

"No, but Ivy and Heather and me are still trying to talk her into playing. Coach says he'll find room for her if she wants to play."

Mama sits back down across from me. I can tell she didn't get much sleep. She has the prettiest green eyes. But today there's still that touch of redness in them. Not as red as her hair, though. Mama is so pretty with her green eyes and red hair. I'll never be as pretty as she is, but I'm so lucky I have hair like hers.

I know some girls who say they wish they weren't redheads. I don't understand how they can't not love their red hair. Just looking at Mama makes me feel good about myself, knowing I look a lot like her.

"Ginny's played before, hasn't she?" Mama said. "Don't you play at school, in P.E.?"

"I think that's why she hates baseball."

"Why is that? She's a good athlete. I know she can handle herself on the tennis court. I'm sure she'd be good at baseball, too."

"I know. I think she's afraid she'll get hit by the ball again."

Mama breaks into a smile. "Oh, that's right. I remember."

"I don't think Ginny will ever forget. We were playing in P.E. and the ball hit her right in the mouth. It gave her a bloody lip, and her mouth was swollen for a couple days."

"I shouldn't laugh," Mama says, but I can see she's working hard not to. "I know it wasn't funny to Ginny. But I remember it was the day of your class play. She had the lead."

"Right. And she still says it was one of the worst days of her life. She had to say all her lines through puffy, swollen lips. She was totally embarrassed by how bad she looked, and she didn't think anybody in the audience would be able to understand what she was saying. She felt like she had a mouthful of cotton."

"She did great, though."

"She sure did." I glance at my watch. In fifteen minutes the bus will come. It's only a three or four minute walk to the bus stop, but Ginny and I always like to be a little early. I take a final big swallow of orange juice. "She thinks she did awful, though, and she blames baseball for it."

Mama reaches over and touches my hand. "You've got your work cut out for you, I guess, if you're going to convince Ginny that baseball is fun and safe."

It seems like my morning is never really off to a good start until I feel Mama's touch, when she gives me a hug or touches my hand. This day is off to a great start.

"I guess," I say. "But I like challenges."

"I know you do." Mama's voice softens, and the smile leaves her face. "Challenges make us stronger people. Better people." She quickly wraps both her hands around her coffee cup and says, "Almost time for your bus. You'd better hurry."

"Are you okay, Mama?"

"I'm fine. You have fun at school today. Write something beautiful."

"I'll try."

Maybe today I'll write something I'll be able to let Mama read. I don't dare show her the poem I wrote last night, the "What I remember most" poem. It would make her feel even worse about missing our game.

five

mr. gallagher's class

When school's over at three o'clock half of us rush out to the bus. The rest are picked up by a parent. I sit with Ginny on the bus and tell her how much fun it was today in Mr. Gallagher's class.

"He let us read our poems out loud if we wanted to," I say, "but he didn't make us read."

"You read yours, didn't you?" Ginny says.

"No way."

I like it that Mr. Gallagher doesn't force anybody to read their poems. I mean, I don't mind writing personal stuff, but I don't want the whole class to hear it. That's why I didn't read my poem about getting the winning hit and Mama and Dad not coming to the game. I didn't mind if Mr. Gallagher saw it, but no way was I going to read it out loud.

"You should read them," Ginny says. "I thought everything you wrote was great. You should let the class hear them."

"Some of them are too personal. I can't read those."

Mr. Gallagher said he was going to type some of our poems and make copies so we could enjoy the poems written by other class members and learn from them. He said he wouldn't type the poems that had NO written at the top of the page.

I made sure that most of mine had a big NO at the top.

I tell Ginny how Mr. Gallagher had us write a lot of other things today. Some were three-line poems. He told us not to use rhyme. He said our poems were a kind of haiku, but that we didn't have to use the 5–7–5 syllable pattern that a traditional haiku uses.

I wrote about a girl on the tennis court.

On the green tennis court
Yellow fuzzy balls skip
Into the twang of catgut strings.

The neatest thing was: when Mr. Gallagher came around to see our work he said he liked it! He said, "You have some good images—your colors, the sound of the ball." He liked my verb 'skip.' He said, "Some writers would have said 'bounce'; 'skip' is a more unusual choice. When you're writing, try to come up with the unusual. Don't always use the same words everybody else would use." Then he asked me, "Do you play much tennis?"

"Some," I said. "Mostly with my family or my friend Ginny. My mom played in college, and she taught me how to play."

"Kate's good," Allison said. "She could play in tournaments if she wanted to."

I like Allison a lot. She's a year older than me and we go to different schools, so I don't get a chance to spend much time with her, but we go to the same church. She's been in the same youth group as Ginny and me for a couple years. It was nice of Allison to say that, but I don't think I'm that good.

"Pretty impressive, Kate," Mr. Gallagher said. "I hope you'll write some more poems about tennis." Then he said, "That's something I hope each of you will do: write about the things that interest you most. You all have talents and interests that would be fun for others to read about. That's what poetry is all about—sharing with others how you feel about things."

Then some other kids read more three-liners. I wasn't surprised at the poem Allison read. She titled it, "My Favorite Book."

God's word beside my pillow
Filling me with peace
God's words of peace for me.

One thing about Allison, she's not afraid or embarrassed to let people know how she feels about God. I
wish I could be that open. I go to Sunday School and
church every week. I'm active in all the church's youth
activities. And I love God. I really do. But I pretty
much keep how I feel about him to myself. I admire
Allison for being strong enough to let people know
how she feels, especially when she gets teased by some
people for being "goody-goody." It doesn't even seem
to bother her when people say that about her.

Another thing about Allison, she never puts others
down if they don't believe the way she does about God.

Mr. Gallagher had us write a lot of other things,
not just the three-line poems. Every few minutes he'd
switch to something new, so class never got boring. He
read some of his own poems, and he read poems by
Robert Frost and Shel Silverstein and some other poets
I'd never heard of. But the way he read made all of
them sound good.

The final poem we worked on before the class
ended for the day was what Mr. Gallagher called an
Expansion Poem. We had to take one of our three-
line poems and make it longer by adding details to
it. We could describe the place in more detail or add

other people or show more of the action. We could tell how the people were feeling. We could make it into a little story if we wanted to.

I'd written six different three-line poems, and the one I decided to expand was my tennis poem.

On the green tennis court
Yellow fuzzy balls skip
Into the twang of catgut strings.
We dance to the music,
My mother and me, together
On one side of the net.
Across the net my dad and brother
Stumble amid the sound of laughter
Trying to return our powerful shots.
Finally, they sprawl down in defeat,
Faces red and puffing on the green court,
While Mama and me, tanned and fresh,
Barely breathing hard at all,
Jump the net to congratulate them
For a good try.

Well, that's not exactly how our tennis matches always turn out. Mama and I aren't always partners, and I don't always win. But Mr. Gallagher said a poem doesn't have to be true. A poem is one time when it's all right to lie, he said. Except he didn't call it lying; he called it "changing reality." The main thing, he said, is that you should just have fun writing a poem.

I had fun writing my tennis story poem, even though it wasn't a "beautiful" poem like Mama suggested. Even so, I think it's one she'll like when I show it to her.

"Hey," I say to Ginny, "I've been rattling on about my day. Tell me about yours. What was your class like?"

Ginny laughs. "Oh Romeo, Romeo! Wherefore art thou Romeo?" she says in a real dramatic voice. Then, in her normal voice, she says, "I'm glad your class was fun. You know about *Romeo and Juliet*, by Shakespeare?"

"I've heard of it."

"Well, this afternoon I got to play a scene as Juliet."

She bus pulls up, and as we walk up the aisle toward the front of the bus, Ginny is already on stage: "What's in a name? That which we call a rose by any other name would smell as sweet."

One of the girls up ahead turns around and smiles. "Go girl!" she calls out.

I can't even begin to picture myself on stage speaking lines like Ginny does. I'm happier than ever I'm in Mr. Gallagher's creative writing class.

six

a change of plans

The bus stop is almost halfway between our two houses. Instead of going our separate ways, we both walk to Ginny's. Mama has arranged for me to stay with her every afternoon until the three-week class is over. Mama and Dad both work until about five o'clock and they don't want me and Ken home alone all that time. They've arranged for Ken to spend the day at one of several places: the ballfield, the swimming pool, or a friend's house. Mama and Dad have a permanent arrangement with Mrs. Loden from across the street to be Ken's "daytime mom." Ken has his own cell phone and has to let her know where he is, even if he's at home.

Ken doesn't like that arrangement much, but Dad

told him, "Think about it. It's better than the alternative." Which would be for him to have an actual babysitter. Ken realizes he has more freedom this way. And the thought of him having a babysitter makes him so mad his ears turn red.

Mrs. Loden is about my grandmother's age. I don't know if they're paying her or she does it just because she's a nice neighbor and hardly ever goes anywhere.

A few minutes after I get to Ginny's I get a phone call from Mama.

"How was school?" she says.

"Great! Today was the most fun yet."

"I'm glad," she says, but her voice sounds kind of funny. Not funny funny, but different somehow. There's something in her voice that makes me think something's wrong. "I'd like you to come home now," she says. "I would have called you earlier, but this was something your dad and I decided on at the last minute."

"What's up?"

"A picnic. The four of us are driving to the lake for a picnic."

She means Corbin Lake. It's only about ten miles away. We go there to swim a lot.

"Now? Aren't you at work?"

"You dad and I both got off early today, just so we could have this picnic."

It seems a little strange to me. They hardly ever leave work early. Yesterday she was too sick to come to my game, and today she leaves work to go to a picnic. That's not like Mama.

"Can I bring Ginny?"

"Not today," she says. "Next time, for sure."

Things are getting weirder all the time. She usually doesn't mind if I bring Ginny along whenever we go somewhere.

When I tell Ginny and her mom that Mama wants me at home, Ginny says, "Too bad. I was going to play my new Lisalette Krebs CD for you."

I don't tell her about the picnic. She might not understand why she's not invited. Since I don't really understand either, I decide it's better not to even tell her.

I run home fast. Dad is tying a rope around the inner tubes we always take to the lake with us. They're big—too big to fit inside our van. Mama is carrying out a cooler. I can guess what's inside: hamburgers, hot dogs, tomatoes, relish, onions, jello squares, cans of soda. I would guess potato salad, but probably not today. If Mama just got home from work, she probably wouldn't have had time to make it. Along with the marshmallows, Ken is carrying a bag of potato chips.

Dad must have seen the puzzled look on my face. He says, "It's too nice a day to spend working."

I'm not used to seeing Dad dressed like this on a weekday. He almost always wears a suit, or at least a pair of slacks and nice shirt and a tie and sport coat. Today he's wearing faded blue jeans, sneakers, and a tattered t-shirt he picked up at a yard sale. The shirt is gray with the word DOGS in red print. On the front of the shirt are faces of four dogs. The back of the shirt shows the same four dogs from behind.

"Hurry up," Ken urges. "I can hardly wait to get to the water."

Dad laughs. "And that food, I imagine."

"That, too," Ken says. He says to me, "Come on, slowpoke."

It's a strange day. But all I say is, "Do I have time to go to the bathroom and get my swimming suit?"

Mama smiles. "Of course. The lake will wait for us."

I go inside. From the living room window I see the three of them outside our van, and it looks like a normal family outing.

Except it sure doesn't feel like one.

seven

the picnic

Three things I like best about Corbin Lake: it's close enough to home that we can go there a lot, it has a sandy beach and sandy bottom that makes it nicer than lakes with sharp rocks that poke your feet, and the water is almost the perfect temperature in the summer. On a hot day like today, you want to stay in forever.

What's even better about today is it's a weekday and we're about the only ones here. We have the lake practically to ourselves. On summer weekends it's pretty crowded.

We float for awhile on our inner tubes. Then Dad calls out, "Time for a game of Keep-Away Frisbee!"

We take the inner tubes up by our picnic table and divide into teams. Dad and I are on one team,

Ken and Mama on the other. We're all good swim-
mers, so the teams are evenly matched. In the shallow water I love to crouch and time my leap so I
can shoot up over Ken's back and snatch the Frisbee
inches before he can grab it.

After fifteen minutes of Keep-Away and the joy
of dunking Ken at least a dozen times, we all swim
out to the raft.

"When do we eat?" Ken says. "That made me
hungry. Especially with Kate landing on my back all
the time and practically drowning me."

"That's just because you don't have my strength
and stamina," I say. "You can't keep up with me."

"Yeah? Race you around the raft!"

We jump off. Ken gets the inside track. The only
thing that keeps him from winning is that I grab his
foot on the final turn, pulling him under. While he
gasps for air, I swim to victory.

"Not fair!" he protests. He pleads his case to
Mama and Dad. "You saw it!"

Mama smiles. "Do you need an umpire?"

I know how an umpire would have called it. "I
guess not," I say. "I guess you might have won, little
brother, in a fair race."

"Might have? I was so far ahead, it was awesome!"

"Well," Mama says, "after that awesome victory,
I guess you deserve some dinner. I'll swim back and

get it ready."

"I'll help," I tell her.

"No, that's okay," Dad says. "I'll help your mother. I know about your help. You'd help by eating all the marshmallows. Untoasted. And not have any room left for hamburgers." He winks and dives off the raft.

"There's always room for hamburgers!" I call after him.

Ken and I sit on the edge of the raft, dangling our feet into the water. The water seems cooler at the raft's edge, but not cold. Just right. I watch Mama spreading food on a tablecloth. Dad stands next to the grill.

"What do you think's wrong?" I ask.

"What do you mean?"

"You saw them last night. And this morning. Mama seemed ... different."

"Different? You're crazy." Ken lifts his right foot and slaps it down onto the water, splashing drops upward into a miniature fountain.

"Maybe," I say. "But I'm worried about them."

"You always worry too much. Everything's cool. We're having a picnic. I mean, they got off work early just so we could come here."

"That's what I mean. Doesn't that seem strange to you? Have they ever taken off work before so we could go on a picnic?"

Ken's only answer is a shrug.

Mama waves to us, and we dive from the raft and swim to shore. We learned to swim almost before we could walk. We've always done athletic things together as a family—softball, tennis, swimming, golf. I have good friends I like to be with, but my favorite times are when our family does things together. I'm lucky. Not many of my friends can say that about their parents, except maybe Ginny.

I know it's silly to worry when there probably isn't anything wrong, but I still can't shake the feeling that things aren't right.

eight

the talk

After we finish eating, we all sprawl out on a big blanket Dad brought, one big enough for all four of us with room still left over. I'm stuffed from all the burgers and marshmallows. I don't know what I was so worried about. The day has been great. I can't imagine how it could be better. For one thing, class was really fun. The weather is perfect. We had the lake to ourselves earlier. Since we got out of the water a few others have come, but it's still not very crowded.

Today's picnic was something I didn't expect, but it's nice that Mama and Dad came home from work early so we could all come here. Ken has the right idea. Why worry when there's nothing to worry about?

I haven't written my new poems for Monday yet, but I'm not worried about that, either. I have the whole weekend and I know I can get at least two or three new poems out of what's happened at this picnic. I already have one in mind, how a big army of ants dropped down on our food. That didn't happen, but I think it will make a good poem. I think I'll write another one that is true, about my race with Ken.

Dad interrupts my thoughts. He clears his throat and says, "Kate. Ken. We have some bad news. We've wondered about the best way to tell you." He pauses. Then he says, "But there isn't a best way."

I suddenly feel chilled all over, like somebody poured ice water over me. That great feeling I had a few seconds ago is gone. It's like somebody just flicked a switch. There's something in his voice I've never heard before. Something that scares me.

I look at Dad, but I can't make eye contact with him. His eyes don't stay on any one thing. They move back and forth from the ground, the lake, the picnic table. Everywhere but us. I try to imagine what the bad news is. How bad can it possibly be? It can't be a divorce. A lot of my classmates' parents have gotten divorced, but I know mine never will. They love each other too much.

I hope we're not going to move. I've lived in the same house practically forever. All my good friends live close by. I wonder if something's happened to Grandma or Grandpa.

"We don't know quite how to tell you, and we thought being together here at the lake might be the best way ..."

Now I'm really scared by the way his eyes look, by the trouble he's having trying to talk. I see Mama's eyes meet Dad's, and I see her give a quick nod of her head.

I can only stare at her. I feel Ken beside me. I can't see his face, but I can hear his silence. It's like he's stopped breathing. Or maybe it's me who has stopped breathing. I feel almost like I'm a dream. I wait for someone to say something. Maybe when somebody finally speaks again, I'll wake up and whatever Dad had said about bad news will be nothing more than the end of a bad dream.

I'm surprised to hear my own voice: "What bad news?"

Mama's body seems to stiffen. "I have cancer."

The word pounds me like a tidal wave. I feel myself drowning. I take a deep breath, trying to stay above the water.

I can't even force myself to speak. Then I hear Ken's voice. It seems far away. "Hannah, from my class at school—her dad had cancer last year, and he's fine now."

Silence seems to grow into an ocean, and I feel myself in the middle of it, surrounded by waves twenty feet high.

Mama is sitting on the blanket now. She's leaning against Dad. His arm is around her shoulder. She looks the same as she's always looked. She doesn't look sick. How can you have cancer and not look sick?

"Your father and I agreed that we shouldn't keep anything from you," Mama says. "You're old enough now. You should know everything, so we can face it together."

I want to scream for her to stop. I know somehow that anything else she might say will be too terrible to hear. But the scream won't come out.

"The cancer is ... advanced," Mama says. "The doctor doesn't think it will get better." Her voice is calm and gentle. Her voice doesn't match the words.

I feel Mama's arms around me. I don't even know whether I moved toward her or if she moved toward me. It doesn't matter. All that matters is that I'm in Mama's warm embrace.

"Will you have to have an operation to get rid of the cancer?" Ken asks. His voice seems louder than usual.

Dad clears his throat. "The doctor talked about all the possible treatments. But your mother's cancer is ... is just too far advanced. There's nothing ... the doctor said ..." His voice cracks and he turns away.

Mama says, "There's nothing surgery can do."

"What about ... chemo-something?" Ken asks. "That will make you better, won't it? That's what Hannah's dad had." He talks really fast. I've never heard him talk so fast.

"I wish it could," Mama says. She releases her hold on me. She shakes her head ever so slightly. She reaches out to touch Ken's hair, but he twists his head away.

"Chemotherapy and radiation treatments are still an option," Dad said, "but ..." His voice trails off again. He doesn't seem able to finish a sentence.

I'm glad he doesn't finish his thought. I don't want to hear the words. I don't want to hear any more about the cancer. Not ever again. If I don't hear any more, then maybe none of it's true. Maybe it's all just been something I dreamed. Maybe this whole afternoon is just something I dreamed.

Mama's cheek is pressed against mine. I feel tears, and I know I'm not dreaming the tears. They're real. What I don't know is if they're hers or mine.

"I know this is sudden," Mama says, "but we just found out for sure from the doctor yesterday. We've never kept secrets from each other. And it wouldn't be fair to any of us to keep this from you."

I finally force myself to speak. "Maybe he's

wrong. The doctor."

Dad moves to Mama. She releases me, and Dad takes her hand and pulls her toward him. She almost floats into his arms. Ken is still standing away from us, out of everybody's reach. "It's not just one doctor," Dad says. "They've run tests and done consultations."

Everything seems to be frozen in place: the sun's reflection sticking to the still lake, a diver in mid-air off the wooden raft, a small child with one foot raised at the edge of the water. It seems like forever before I'm able to find my voice. "You'll be all right, Mama." My voice sounds small to my ears. I don't even recognize it as my own. I can barely hear my own words. No one says anything. I wait for her to agree with me, but she doesn't.

"How can the ... it be so bad?" I say. "You haven't even been sick. Just last week we played that great tennis match, three long sets. How many games?" I mentally calculate the scores. "Thirty. You couldn't have done thirty games if you were sick."

Mama moves from Dad's arms and puts out a hand toward me. She stops and stares out toward the lake. I look out and try to see what she's seeing. The diver is in the water now. The small boy is still dipping his foot into the water with his mother right beside him.

"At first I thought the doctor must be wrong,"
Mama says. "I've been having some pain lately, but it
hasn't been bad. I just thought it was a combination of
too much exercise and getting older."

"You're not old, Mom," Ken says.

She smiles and I feel a quick burst of anger. What
does she have to smile about?

"Well," she says, "thirty-four isn't old, of course.
But it's not like being twenty, when I played tennis in
college. Except for the exhaustion of healthy exercise, I've never really known what pain is. As you
get older, and you start getting little aches, you think
they're just part of aging. I guess that's why I didn't
go to the doctor sooner."

No one says anything, and I wonder if everyone
is thinking what I am. I want to scream the words,
but I keep them to myself: If you had gone to the
doctor earlier, they would have found the cancer and
they'd be able to make you well again! How could
you not go earlier?

But I'm glad I don't say it. It wouldn't do anybody any good.

I run toward the lake, almost knocking over the
little boy who's wading in the shallow water. I start
swimming toward the raft, water splashing against
my hot tears. I don't look back to see if anyone is
coming after me.

When I get to the raft, I see them still sitting on

the blanket, even Ken. I wonder what they're talking about now. Is there more about the cancer they're telling Ken?

If there is, I'm glad I don't have to hear.

nine

the place for love

Friday night at our house is usually popcorn and movie night. Mama and Dad pick out a DVD that we can watch together. Sometimes instead of watching movies we play games like Monopoly or Scattergories or UNO or Outburst. And a bunch of others. We have some video games—my favorites are the ones that require a lot of physical competition—but we play a lot of board games with dice or cards. Dad's kind of a collector of games.

Our Friday night family time has been a tradition as long as I can remember. But I don't want to leave my room. I can't pretend nothing has changed.

I can smell the popcorn. Usually the popcorn smell makes my mouth start to water, and I can't wait to feel that salty, buttery taste on my tongue.

But now it doesn't even smell good to me.

There's a tap at my bedroom door. "Kate, can I come in?"

I wipe my tears and sit up in bed. "Yes, Mama."

She's holding a bowl of popcorn and an orange soda, my favorite drink. "I thought you might like these." She puts them down on my desk and sits beside me on my bed.

I throw my arms around her. "Oh Mama! I don't want you to be sick! I don't want you to be!"

"I know, dear. But I want you to know something. Something very important." She touches my cheek lightly with the back of her fingers. I try to fight back tears, but it's no use. I know that the world will never be a happy place if Mama isn't here to sit beside me and touch my cheek.

"When the doctor first told me, I was certain he'd made a mistake. I wasn't feeling bad enough to be as sick as he said I was. It took me awhile to accept the fact that I do have cancer. And not only that, but that they probably won't be able to cure it."

I look into Mama's eyes. I've always been so proud to have the kindest, prettiest mother of any of my friends. But now, it's as if I'm seeing her for the first time. It's as if I've never really looked at her before. It isn't that she's changed—it's still hard to believe she's really sick. But what's different is that I realize I've always taken her for granted, thinking that she'll always be here, forever and ever.

Mama squeezes my hand. "Then I got angry," she says. "I thought about how unfair it is that I should get cancer. I've always exercised. I've made sure to eat healthy foods. I've never smoked or taken drugs. How could it happen to me? I've always thought I'd live to see you and Ken grow up and get married and have a career ..."

Suddenly she pulls me close to her, and I can feel tears that I know are hers.

"It's okay, Mama. It's okay to cry." Because I'm crying too and we're holding tight to each other.

Mama wipes away her tears, and mine too, and she smiles. She tries to, anyway. At least she does a better job of it than I do. I don't know if I'll ever smile again. "I'm sorry, Kate. I didn't intend to cry. I was going to talk to you about how we all have to be brave and accept whatever happens as God's will. But it's still hard for me to accept."

She reaches for the dish of popcorn and hands it to me. "Here. I popped the yellow popcorn tonight, especially for you."

I don't feel much like thinking about popcorn, but I take the dish and nibble at a couple of kernels. "Thanks, Mama," I whisper.

"The one thing I most want to tell you," she says, "Is that I'm not afraid of the future. Oh, I'd like to live to be an old lady with a bunch of grandchildren running around my house." She reaches out for a handful of popcorn. "There's a poem called 'Birches.' Robert Frost wrote it. In it he said, 'Earth's the right place for love; I don't know where it's likely to go better.' I've always liked that line because I've been so lucky: my life has always been filled with love. I've known the special love of our friends from church, our special church family. My parents and brothers and sisters are all close. Your father is the most wonderful man in the world, and he chose me for his wife. And I have the two most terrific children that any mother can have. No one who has known the love I have would want to leave that love behind."

"You won't have to," I blurt out. "They'll come up with a cure. I know they will."

"Maybe they will," Mama says. "I pray they will. But I know this: the time I have left on this earth, whether it's months or years, will be filled with a far deeper love than most people have ever known. I realize how very, very lucky I am."

What Mama says reminds me of a movie we'd all watched together a few months ago. It was an old movie about a baseball player who was dying, and he said he was the luckiest man on the face of the earth. I wondered how he could consider himself lucky. And now Mama is saying almost the same thing.

"Oh, I love you, Mama. I do!" I hug her again, tight. I don't ever want to let her go.

"I know you do. You're the light of my life. You and Ken and your father. I couldn't face this without all of you. And I need you all to help me, help us all, fill every day with happy thoughts. While we still have the gift of life, we can't waste our time mourning or feeling sad. Each day is a precious gift, a gift from God."

She stands and walks to the window and brushes the drapes aside. It isn't dark yet. The last sliver of sun has left the sky a gorgeous purplish-pink.

I can't help but think about how amazing the sky looks. It should be black. Or gray. Why would God make the sky so pretty when he's doing this awful thing to Mama?

"Just look how pretty the sky is. I think God's doing it on purpose, to remind us how much beauty there is in the world."

I gasp. Out loud. It's like Mama is reading my mind.

"Always see the beauty," she says. "Not the pain. Not the ugliness. I realize this is all new to you, to all of us. You'll need time. We all will. But try to remember what I've said. Each day is a gift. I've been lucky enough to live for more than twelve thousand days. I figured it up today. I did. And almost every one of those days has been special. So full of joy. There are a lot of people who've lived to be seventy or eighty years old who haven't seen anywhere near the number of wonderful days I've experienced already. Remember God's gift of giving us so many days of joy and love. Okay, Kate? Try to remember."

I take a deep breath. "I'll try, Mama."

Her lips brush my forehead. "If you want to come out, we'll be starting a movie in a few minutes that you might like."

"I don't think so, Mama. Not right now."

"I love you, Kate." Mama closes the door softly behind her.

"I know, Mama," I whisper to the empty room. I lie down and stare at the ceiling.

I keep thinking about all the things Mama said. I lie there without moving until all the ice has melted in my glass of orange soda.

ten

the death poem

On the bus to school Ginny keeps asking me
what's wrong. I finally shout, "Nothing's wrong,
all right? Just stop asking!" I pull a book from my
backpack and pretend to read.

I don't even have to glance their way to know
the two girls sitting across the aisle are looking at
me. Ginny doesn't say anything. I feel terrible about
shouting at her. I want to apologize, but I can't. If
I do, that'll just get her talking again. I don't want
to have to say anything. I just want the bus to get
to school. Maybe once it's there I can lose myself
in whatever Mr. Gallagher has us do and block out
yesterday from my mind.

I know I'll have to tell Ginny about Mama sometime, but I'm not ready to talk about it. I wouldn't

know what to say. I didn't even want to come to school today, but that would have taken even more explaining. Besides, I know it would have upset Mama if I'd quit my creative writing class in the first week.

Mr. Gallagher starts class the same way he does every day, by giving us what he calls a "starter activity." He gives us a lot of them. They're different ways to help us get those first words on the page. He says that for most writers the hardest thing is staring at a blank page, not knowing how to start. He says that once we have a few words on the page, the rest comes easier.

Today nothing comes easy. We work for an hour and a half. During that time he gives us four different "starter activities." I try all of them, but none of them are good. They're just words. They don't mean anything. When he asks the class to read, I don't read any of mine.

Mr. Gallagher told us the first day of class that we should never throw away anything we write. But I don't have anything on my paper today worth keeping. I just keep thinking, "What am I doing here? I should be with Mama." But if I weren't here, I couldn't be with Mama anyway. She's at work. I don't understand why she's still going to work. She should stay home with us. If she were home, I wouldn't be coming to school today. There's no way she could make me.

Mr. Gallagher holds up a blank sheet of paper. He says, "The main joy of any artist is to take this blank sheet of paper and bring to it something that would not exist except for the imagination and talent and craft and soul of the artist. Poets write poems about every subject, and to fit any mood, happy or sad or angry or lonely." He holds up a book. "I've been reading you some of Shel Silverstein's poems. He wrote a lot of silly poems. He did a great job of reading them, too. I'd like to play part of a CD of him reading some of his own poems. You can see that it can be fun not only to write poems, but to read them out loud."

Shel Silverstein's voice is weird. Weird-funny. I've never heard anybody who sounds like he does. It's impossible not to laugh, and I do, right along with everybody else. He reads four or five poems before I even realize I'm laughing.

Suddenly something in my head blocks out Silverstein's words. I see Mama's face and I remember her words from last night. I know what she said about being happy and enjoying every minute, but I can't do it. I don't have the right. I feel like screaming. Mama's dying and I'm laughing. What kind of person am I? Mama said she wants me to be happy, but she'd be disappointed in me if she knew I was laughing right now. I know she would. Laughing is almost like saying I'm not sad about what's happening.

I try not to listen to the rest of the CD. I'm afraid all the poems will be funny, and I don't want to hear anything that might make me laugh again. Not today.

Mr. Gallagher says, "Free writing time. I'm going to give you fifteen minutes to write. It can be the first draft of a poem, but it doesn't have to be. It can be the start of a story, or it can just be a few sentences. It can be silly or serious. Maybe you heard something in one of Shel Silverstein's poems that will give you an idea for some writing of your own."

"What if we can't think of anything?" Jill Cannon asks.

"Then just write a single word," Mr. Gallagher says. "Maybe a noun. Let's say you write the word 'dog.' You could think about a dog of yours or maybe a friend's dog. Think about something it did or what it looks like. Whatever word you begin with, just ask yourself 'when' and 'who' and 'where' and 'what happened.' Don't worry about an ending, just start with a word or idea and see where it takes you."

"What if we need more time?" someone asks.

"Don't worry about a finished product. Just write as much as you can. You'll have plenty of time later if you're not finished. You'll have the whole rest of your life to revise."

The whole rest of your life. The words burn in my ears. He talks like that's forever.

"I'm not looking for polished or finished work," he continues. "I'm not even going to collect what you write—that is, unless you want to let me see it. Just write as much as you can. And as I said before, don't ever throw any of your writings away. When you're eighty years old, you should still have everything you've ever written."

Why is it that everything he says today reminds me of Mama? He's talking like everybody will live to be eighty. Well, they won't. Doesn't he know that? Why would it even matter if I write another poem or story if Mama won't be able to read it?

Everybody else is writing, so I take my blank sheet of paper. I don't want him to think anything's wrong. If he did, he might start asking questions, like Ginny did.

I think about some of the things Shel Silverstein wrote about in the poems I'd paid attention to. I write one of the words on my paper. I cross it out and write another. And another. My mind's a blank. All I have on my paper are those three words.

Homework

Bands

Pony

A fourth word pops on my paper. I didn't plan it. It's like it wrote itself. I stare at my paper.

Dying

I bite at my lower lip and my hand starts to move. I watch my pen move across the paper, but I don't pay any attention to what the words are. I don't even think about what I'm writing. It's like my pen has a mind of its own.

When my pen gets tired and stops, I read what's on the page.

Dying

No No No

Stop it! Stop death

I hate it. It isn't fair.

Why do people have to die?

Why? It isn't fair. Isn't there

a way to stop death? To live,

give life, to never stop, never

stop keep going

she's wrong, they're wrong,

the death poem

live until we're eighty,
lies! lies!
everybody will live until 80
sure they will!
and read everything
and play tennis and go swimming
and eat popcorn and play baseball
otherwise why bother waking up
in the morning and listen to people
talk about things they don't know
anything about
about art about creating things
just so they can die someday
nobody knows what will

My pen had stopped writing before it even finished a thought, but I don't have any idea what the
thought even was. All I know is that the words on the
page don't make any sense and that I'll never show
the page to anybody.

I rip it from my notebook and crumple the paper into a little ball and stuff it in my pocket. I pick
up my notebook and walk toward the door. I don't
run. I don't want Mr. Gallagher to think anything's
wrong. But I walk as fast as I can.

I walk all the way to the bleachers next to the baseball diamond behind the school and just stare out at the field. It's not the same field our team played its game on last week—it seems a year ago—but I try to picture my last at-bat. Me getting the hit, Andy sliding across home plate with the winning run, everybody congratulating me. It was such a great time—while it lasted.

"What is it, Kate?"

I look around. It's Mr. Gallagher. "Is something wrong? Anything I can do to help?"

"No," I tell him. "I'm sorry I left the room without permission."

His hand brushes the air as if he's trying to brush away a gnat or something. "Oh, don't worry about that. That's not why I'm here. I just thought you might want to talk."

"There's nothing to talk about."

Mr. Gallagher sits down on the bleachers. Not right next to me, though. There would be room for two or three people to sit between us. I glance toward him. He's staring out toward the field. "One quality that almost all writers have is the ability to feel things deeply," he says. "You're feeling deeply about something right now. It's certainly nothing to be sorry about. Embrace the way you feel. But sometimes it's good to talk those feelings out."

"I hate the way I feel. I wish I couldn't feel

anything."

"Want to tell me about it?"

"No," I say. "I can't."

Out of the corner of my eye, I see Mr. Gallagher nodding. "If you ever do want to talk, I'll be happy to listen. If you feel like coming back to class now, please do. If you want to sit out here, that's okay. And if you'd like for me to stay for awhile, I will."

Then the words just tumble out. "My mother's dying."

I don't plan to do it, but it happens. I take the crumbled paper from my pocket and hand it to him. I don't watch him while he reads it.

"I'm so sorry," he says finally. "Would you like to talk about it?"

"She has cancer. There's nothing they can do about it."

"Oh Kate," he says. "I know that there aren't any words that can help right now. Just know that your friends are always here for you, even though you might not always feel it."

Then he says something that surprises me. It sounds like something Mama might say. He says, "Your love will be your strength."

eleven

fog

It's Friday. The second week of class is almost over, but I honestly can't remember much about the week, about what happened either in or out of class. Everything's cloudy, almost like I've been walking around in fog all week. I know I went to school every day. I know I spent the afternoons with Ginny after school. I don't think I yelled at her again, but I also know I didn't tell her about Mama's cancer.

I know I went home at five o'clock every day. I know our baseball team played two games. I think we won both of them. No, I know we did. I remember that. I don't remember the scores, though. And I don't think I did anything especially good. I didn't get a game-winning hit. I would have remembered. I'm pretty sure of that. I do remember that I didn't want to play. I only played because Mama and Dad were going to be at the games. They expected me to play. I couldn't not play without a good reason, and I didn't really have one. Not one they'd understand anyway.

Details. I remember that word from our first week of class. Mr. Gallagher used it a lot. Details. They're the difference, he said, between just an average piece of writing and a good one. Details. The good writer lets us see everything, not just with our eyes but with all our senses.

He might have used the word this week, too. He probably did. I don't remember many details of the past few days. Every day has been pretty much the same. I get up every morning. I sleepwalk through the day. I'm anxious for night to come so I can go to sleep. A real sleep, not just a daytime one. When I'm asleep I don't have to think. I don't have to remember. Except in dreams. But my nighttime dreams haven't been nearly as bad as my daytime ones.

We'll only have one hour of class left after our afternoon break. I'm sitting here watching our class play volleyball. Some of them tried to get me to play, but I don't feel like it. It's almost like my body's numb. I don't feel like doing anything.

Mr. Gallagher is playing on one of the teams. He calls to me, "Are you sure you don't want to play? We can use you on our team."

I tell him no, and he doesn't tell me I have to play.

I watch the ball go back and forth over the net. I watch Allison jump up to spike the ball. She comes back down and ends up on her knees in the sand. She reaches for her ankle.

"Are you okay?" Mr. Gallagher asks.

Allison bounces right back up. "Sure. Just twisted my ankle a bit. Nothing serious, but I think I'll sit out for awhile." She comes over and flops down beside me.

"You didn't sprain it, did you?" I ask.

"No, just twisted it a little. It'll be okay in a minute." She bends her leg and reaches out to rub her ankle. "I haven't heard you read your work in class yet."

I shrug. "I don't have anything worth reading."

"I don't believe that. You write really well."

"Not like you. I love your poems." We're sitting on sandy ground next to the volleyball court. I pick up a handful of sand and let it sift through my fingers.

"Thanks," she says. "I really love our class. I've been writing poems since I was in third grade, but I've never had as good a teacher as Mr. Gallagher."

He's up at the net. The ball comes to him. He could easily spike it and win the point, but he tips it to Miranda. She's too short to spike the ball, but she manages to get it back over the net. I've noticed that Mr. Gallagher doesn't take advantage of his height or the fact that he's a lot better player than anybody

75

else. He doesn't try to win points outright, he just tries to set up other players.

"I like him," I say. "It's not his fault ..." I was going to say it wasn't his fault I didn't write good poems. Even though I meant it about my poems being bad, I stop. I don't want Allison to think I'm fishing for a compliment or anything like that.

"I was talking to him at lunch today," Allison said. "He told me that one of the things he plans to have us do is write collaborative poems."

"What are those?"

"He said next week one of the things he's going to do is have us choose a partner and write some poems with them. Two people working on one poem. I thought it would be fun if the two of us paired up. That is, if you wouldn't mind."

All of a sudden something clicks in my mind. It all seems too much of a coincidence. I can't help but wonder. Mr. Gallagher and I haven't talked about Mama since that one day. I'm pretty sure he hasn't told anybody what we talked about. No one in the class seems to know about her cancer. Now he told Allison about the collaborative poems. She twists her ankle and comes to sit by me. And she asks if I will be her partner on the collaborative poem assignment. It's as if Mr. Gallagher is trying to get Allison to talk to me about Mama. Or make it so I'll talk to her. It all seems like a set-up.

fog

"He told you, didn't he?" I whisper. "About my mother."

"Your mother?" Allison says. She looks truly surprised. "No. What about her?"

Suddenly, I can't stop tears from burning my eyes. I push myself to my feet and start to run.

twelve

church pew

I end up at the same bleachers where I sat the day I talked to Mr. Gallagher about Mama. I don't know why I came here; it wasn't on purpose.

I don't even know why I got up and ran from Allison. It's not something I planned.

Maybe it's because deep down I must have hoped Allison would follow me. Maybe the reason I've been walking in a fog all week is because I've kept everything locked inside me. I haven't talked to anybody about Mama because I don't know how to without crying. Or screaming. I just feel so sad all the time. And so angry. I don't understand how God could do something like this.

So I'm not really surprised when Allison sits down beside me. I even feel relieved. God is such an important part of Allison's life I think maybe she can explain it to me. Maybe she has some answers.

Even before she says anything I blurt out that Mama has cancer and the doctors says there's no cure.

I'm not crying anymore. I feel as if a big weight has been lifted from me. I stare out at the field. I know it seems strange to say this, but I almost feel the way I do when I'm in church. Every time I go to church and settle on a church pew with a hymnbook in front of me and look around at the stained glass windows and the large gold cross I always get this warm, comforting feeling.

That's almost what I feel now. It's as if this bleacher I'm sitting on is a church pew. I feel comforted with Allison beside me. She says, "Oh Kate." Then she wraps an arm around me and pulls me close to her.

I can't help but think of the words I've heard in Sunday School Class so often: "The loving arms of Jesus."

Then I feel myself stiffen. Where have Jesus' loving arms been? These are the arms of a girl in my class. A human's arms. How can it be that she can give me comfort and Jesus can't? Where is he? Where is God when I need him? No, not me. It's not me who needs him. It's Mama. She's the one that needs him now more than ever. He can cure the cancer if he wants to. Mama's such a good person. She's always been faithful to God. She doesn't deserve to have this cancer. Where has God gone? Why has he deserted her? Why has he deserted us all?

I pull away and shout, "I hate God! I hate him!" I slam my fist down against the bleachers. I want it to hurt. Maybe the pain will somehow help me forget my other pain. But it doesn't. It just make a dull thud.

"How can God let this happen?" I cry. "Tell me! You're always talking about how good God is. Tell me how a god that's good can do this?"

I wait for an argument from Allison. I expect her to try to justify God's goodness, even though I know she can't.

She doesn't say anything. I see her eyes mist over as she reaches out and pulls me to her. I rest my head on her shoulder and start to sob. I feel her touch as she gently caresses my hair.

thirteen

letting ginny know

After talking to Allison, I know now that I'm ready to tell Ginny. But not here. Not on the bus with all the other kids around.

"Something's wrong," she says. "I know it. Please tell me. You've been acting strange all week. I'm your best friend. Whatever it is, you can tell me. I want to help."

"I know," I say. "But not now. Not here. Later."

I stare at the back of the seat in front of us until I feel the pull of Ginny's eyes. I finally look over at her. "Today," she says. "This afternoon."

I nod. "Yes," I say. "This afternoon."

The bus is full of talking and laughing, just like every day. But there's only silence between Ginny and me the rest of the way home.

I know Ginny is keeping quiet on purpose, waiting for me to speak first. I don't say anything until we're in her back yard.

I say, "I've wanted to talk to you, but I couldn't. I didn't know how. I didn't know what to say."

"It's something terrible," Ginny says quietly. "I know it is. Or else you would have told me already. I've been trying to figure out what it is. The worst thing I can think of is that you're moving away. I don't think I could stand it if you were moving."

A week ago if Mama or Dad had told me we had to move, I would have said just what Ginny did. I couldn't have imagined anything more horrible. Now if only Mama would say that her cancer is cured but we have to move away I think I'd jump up and down and clap my hands and say, "Oh, that's the best news ever!"

We're sitting in Ginny's backyard swings. Her dad built the set years ago, when she was four or five years old. Now we're almost too big for them. I push off with my feet and start to swing. Ginny pushes off too, and soon we're side by side, swinging higher and higher. The breeze on my face feels good. I'm swinging so high I can look straight up at a big fluffy cloud. It's so pretty, stuck up against a clear blue sky.

I have to close my eyes to speak the words. "We're not moving away. Mama's dying."

I open my eyes. I see that Ginny has jerked on

the chains of the swing and is coming to a stop. I
slow my swing down and come to a stop beside her.
She doesn't say anything. I don't either. I can hear
her breathing, though. It's like the whole world has
suddenly become silent. No sounds of cars. No birds.
No doors slamming. No babies crying. No barking
dogs. Only Ginny's breathing.

She's standing in front of me, looking down at
me. I can't see her clearly because my eyes have filled
with tears.

"No," Ginny says. "It's not true."

I pull myself up out of the swing. "She's dying!"
I blurt out the words. I throw my arms around her
neck and bury my head in her shoulder. "She told
us last week. It's cancer. She said there's nothing the
doctors can do."

"I don't believe it. Oh, Kate. Oh, Kate."

And now she's crying too, crying as hard as me.
I don't know if I should have told her. Mama didn't
say I shouldn't tell anybody. That's something we
haven't talked about, if she wanted anybody else to
know. It's just something I couldn't keep inside any
longer. I've felt so alone. I've felt like Mama's de-
serting me. I've felt like God has deserted me. Even
though I've been with Ginny a lot, I've felt so far
away from her because I've had this awful secret I
couldn't bring myself to share.

Now I've told her.

But nothing is better. I still feel deserted by God. I still hate him for letting this happen to Mama.

Nothing can make it better. Except ... now I don't feel quite so alone. I don't have this terrible secret inside me anymore. I know that I have Allison. And even though I feel bad that I've made Ginny cry, I'm really glad I told her.

fourteen

fun in class

Mr. Gallagher told us that most of what we'll be doing this last week of class will be to put together a book of our poems. And of course we'll have to plan our Friday night program. For our part of the program, he said, we'll each read some of our poems.

I don't want to do it, but I know I have to. Mr. Gallagher said it's important that each of us read. "You're each a part of the class, and you all owe it to your classmates to participate. And you owe it to your family. You've all written terrific poems, and they need to hear them."

I don't really think I've written anything terrific yet. I have five more days, though. Maybe I still can.

The fog has lifted. A little bit, anyway. I think

that finally telling Ginny has helped. It was so awful keeping Mama's sickness inside me all that time.

Mama tries to pretend nothing has changed. She doesn't seem sick, and she goes around smiling more than ever. I know what she's trying to do. I know she's trying to make us all feel better.

I try, for Mama's sake, to smile too. I went to church yesterday, like always, and I sat there with Mama and Dad and Ken and tried to sing the hymns. But when we sang "'Tis So Sweet to Trust in Jesus" I couldn't do it. I just couldn't. I listened to the words and found that I couldn't sing them. I didn't believe them. I'd be singing a lie. I heard everybody else singing the chorus: "Jesus, Jesus, how I trust him! How I've proved him o'er and o'er!"

It's not true. I don't trust him. Not now. Not after what he's let happen to Mama. I just stood there and watched Mama singing those words. Her eyes were bright and her face was glowing. Like she really believed those words!

The only thing I could do was whisper a silent prayer: "I want to trust you, Jesus. But I can't. Not until you show me that you care about Mama. That you'll make her well again. If you do that I'll sing your praises forever and forever. Please do that, Jesus."

The rest of the day was so great I almost forgot about Mama's sickness. We went to a major league baseball game at Kauffman Stadium. We live less than two hours from there. It's where our favorite team, the Kansas City Royals, play their home games. It's a beautiful ball park. The best thing is, they played the New York Yankees. The Yankees have all this money and can pay their players a lot more than the other teams can. So they have this big advantage. It's especially fun to see our Royals beat the Yankees.

And they did! The game was so exciting that I hardly thought about anything but the game for the whole three hours. We scored a run in the bottom of the tenth inning to win the game. We all left the stadium with more than thirty thousand other fans thinking that all was right with the world.

The Royals winning a game like that over the Yankees made me think that anything is possible. Maybe it was a sign. Maybe from this time on everything will be all right. Maybe, just maybe, Jesus heard my prayer.

And if that wasn't a sign, I got another one when I first got to class today. Allison gave me a poem. She said, "Here's a poem I wrote this weekend. I thought you might want to see it."

The title was "Prayer."

Splashed against December's sky is snow.
The harsh wind peppers it
against my frozen face; and though
I shiver just a tiny bit, I know
that winter's bleakest rage
cannot begin to match the chill
of frozen souls, of my soul
in that icy place I lived
before I knelt to pray.
The snow that whips my wind-raw face
is warmer still than sunlit cold
of every godless yesterday.

I read the poem over and over. What made
me feel just a little discouraged was knowing how
much better Allison is than I am at writing poetry.
What made me feel good was the poem's message. It
seemed to be saying that prayer can help. Oh, I hope
so, I thought. I hope so. I want my frozen soul to
thaw. I do.

"Okay," Mr. Gallagher says. "To start out, we're
going to try something new today. I'm going to have
you pair up with somebody else and write some
poems together. There are different ways this can
work."

I look over at Allison. She points at me and then back at herself. She mouths the words, "You and me."

"One way to do this is for each of you to write your own poem," Mr. Gallagher says. "If you do, then you help each other out with the revision. Go over each poem word by word, line by line. What can be added? Taken out? What words can be changed?" He pauses. He holds his hands in front of him. Palms out. "But we're not going to do that right now."

He picks up a stack of note cards. "Another thing we could do is give each pair of poets some note cards. Each of the cards has a word on the back, words like 'bird,' 'snow,' 'mountain,' 'water,' and so on. You'll use that word to give you an idea for your poem." He spreads his palms again. "But we're not going to do that yet, either."

"The suspense is killing me," Adrian Barrow says. He's kind of the class clown, except he writes really good poems.

"I'm sure you'll survive," Mr. Gallagher says with a smile. "Now there's another way to approach your poem. Each partnership can work on a single poem. Each of you can contribute ideas, lines, images to it. You can build the poem together."

"But we're not going to do that either, I bet," Adrian says.

"You've got me pegged," Mr. Gallagher says.

"What we're going to do is have a little challenge. I'm going to give you a subject to write about. We'll be able to take a look at all the different ways each of the groups writes about the same subject. It's a subject that will be wide-open. It's limited only by your imagination. The subject is, drum roll please . . ."

"Oh, the suspense!" Adrian says.

" . . . months of the year," Mr. Gallagher says.

"Which month?" Kerry Wilson asks.

"Any month," Mr. Gallagher says. "Every month, if you'd like."

"How long should it be?" Kerry asks.

"As long as it needs to be," Mr. Gallagher says. "Just like most of your other poems."

Allison and I sit at a corner table and start to brainstorm. We go through each of the twelve months. We think of things that have happened to us in each of the months. We list things we associate with each of the months. Like for January: snowball fights, ice-skating, school being cancelled, basketball games, colds. Or April: blossoms, green grass, Easter, baseball season, robins, spring rains, spring breezes.

After half an hour we still haven't started our poem, but we have a page full of ideas for dozens of poems. Which isn't all bad, I guess. Mr. Gallagher keeps telling us that the hardest part of writing poems is coming up with ideas.

fun in class

We have plenty of those.

Mr. Gallagher keeps us busy all day. There's no
time to think of anything but poetry. By the time
school's out and I meet Ginny at the bus, Allison
and I have completed the first draft of our month
poem and I've written four new poems of my own.

It's been my best day of writing in three weeks.
Maybe I'll have something good enough to read on
Friday night after all.

fifteen

ginny's news

Mama and Dad both went to work today, so I'm at Ginny's when the phone rings. The second she's done talking she starts squealing and jumping up and down.

"I got it! I got the part!"

I know without her saying any more just what she's talking about. She's been in enough plays you'd think she wouldn't be this excited. But I guess if I kept getting game-winning base hits I'd probably be just as excited as I was the first time. Not that I ever expect to get another game-winning hit.

"The lead?" I say. "Did you actually get ..."

"I did! I did! I get to play Annie!"

Annie is a musical about a girl who grows up in an orphanage run by a mean woman. She's about ten or eleven when she gets picked to spend the Christmas holidays at the mansion of Daddy Warbucks, who I guess was the richest man in the United States. The play takes place a long time ago, like the 1930s or '40s. It's a whole new world for Annie because she's never had anything. Not only that, she's treated like a princess when she's at Daddy Warbucks' mansion, while the woman who runs the orphanage treated all the girls like slaves. It's a really neat play. I know Ginny will be great as Annie.

She auditioned at the Children's Theater for the part a few days after we started at Valley Lakes School. She got a callback last week to come and read for the part again. She said she knows of at least a dozen girls who got callbacks. She said a lot of the others who didn't get picked to play Annie will probably get to play some of the other orphans.

Annie has curly red hair and gets to sing a lot of solos. Ginny doesn't have red hair. I guess she'll have to wear a wig. The hair's not important, though. What's important is that she's a great actress and she can sing. I get goosebumps when she belts out songs like "Tomorrow" and "It's a Hard Knock Life." I could listen to her all day.

She started practicing for the audition a few weeks ago. I've watched the movie with her five or six times, and I know she's watched it by herself a bunch. She's been practicing Annie's songs, too. If you ask me, I think she sounds just as good as the girl who plays Annie in the movie.

I'm really happy for her, but I'm sad, too. Rehearsals start next week. She said they'll be rehearsing three or four nights a week most of the summer to get ready for the September performances. That means I won't see her nearly as much. And there's no chance now of her playing baseball this summer. First of all, she won't have time. Secondly, she'd have a hard time singing with a puffed-up lip if she got hit in the face with a baseball again.

But it'll be so much fun seeing her up on stage.

"Sing 'Tomorrow' for me," I say.

"Now?"

"Will you? Please?"

"Are you sure?"

"I really want to hear it."

"Really?"

"Really, truly."

So she does.

And I get goosebumps all over.

sixteen

poem prayers

When Ginny first said she was going to audition for *Annie*, I'd never seen the movie. Even when we started watching it, I never felt bad for Annie, not even when she was in the orphanage. I mean, the movie is mostly funny. Even though she didn't have any parents and she was treated bad, I never thought about the bad things.

After I found out about Mama's cancer, I started to see the movie in a different way. I know it's only a made-up story, but still, none of the girls had parents. Some of them, like Annie, never knew their parents. But some of them must have known their mama. Now there they are, without any family except the other girls in the orphanage.

If God won't cure Mama's cancer, I'll at least have Dad and Ken. I won't be alone. I won't be sent to an orphanage. But maybe God won't be that mean. He wouldn't. He has to save her. Maybe if I pray harder. Maybe if I can just find the right words, I can convince God to take away her cancer and make her well again.

I take out my notebook. I try to think of what I can say to God to make him listen. I know I don't really have the right to expect him to listen to me. If I were Allison, with her faith, maybe he would.

I start to write. I want it to be a prayer, but it seems to be taking the shape of a poem.

God, are you there?
I just don't see you anywhere.
God, oh God, why don't you care?
What can I do to make you see
Just how much Mama means to me.

No, that's not right. That's not what I mean to say. Don't do it for me, God. Do it for Mama. I'm not important. She is.

When Mr. Stone, the poet, came to my school, he told us to never throw away anything we write. But I take the page from my notebook and crumple it up. I toss it in the waste basket. What I wrote was dumb. It was selfish. Not only that, I kind of sounded like

Dr. Seuss with his silly rhymes. I can't be silly when
I ask God for help.

Besides, when I said he didn't care, that probably
made him mad. It won't help Mama if I make God
mad. I start to write.

God, I know you'll do all you can
To make my mama well again.

I cross out the "again." This prayer will be better if
it doesn't rhyme. I read it over. I don't like either line.
I scribble them out and try again.

God, I know you are good.
I know you can do anything.
It's so easy for you to just reach down
and take the cancer from Mama's body.
Why won't you do that?

I rip the paper from my notebook and ball it up
and slam it down into the wastebasket. I can't stop the
sobs. I fall onto my bed and bury my face in my pillow.
Why can't I do it? Why can't I find the right words?
I'm probably just making things worse by trying to
convince God to help Mama. He hears words all the
time from people who really know how to pray, who
aren't selfish.

Please God. Please don't make Mama suffer

because of my foolish words. She needs your help. She deserves your help.

Suddenly I'm biting my lower lip so hard it hurts. If I make it bleed maybe that will get God's attention. Maybe he'll realize I really care.

But I start to sob again. Because I realize that God has probably already stopped listening.

seventeen

valley lakes program

The auditorium is packed for our program. It's mostly the families of the more than sixty of us who decided to spend three weeks of our summer vacation in the classroom again. The reason for the program is to show the parents what their talented kids have created during the three weeks. "Talented" isn't my word; it's what the director of Valley Lakes says when he talks to the audience at the start of the program.

I wish it were true. I don't feel especially talented. The worst thing is that in a few minutes I'll have to stand up in front of an auditorium full of people and read some of my poems. My stomach is turning somersaults just thinking about it.

Most of us have to perform on stage. The visual arts kids are the only ones who don't. Their art work is in display in the lobby for everybody to look at when they come and go out after the program is over. All the artists have to do is stand beside their work and talk about it if anybody has questions. And of course get their picture taken alongside their work by somebody in their family.

I've been backstage with the rest of my class while the vocal and dance classes went on. It's given me time to get even more nervous.

My class all walks out on stage. We all have to be on stage together while each of us goes up to the microphone to read our poems.

My hands are shaking when I get to the microphone, but I take a deep breath and feel a little better. I manage to get through my first poem okay. It's a tennis poem, "World Class Lob."

My opponent's lob shot
Played with the sun.
It finally turned and sped away,
Back toward where I waited
To punish the ball
For taking so long to arrive.

The sun saw the danger,
rumbled from the sky,
Stuck its blinding rays in my eyes,
Letting the ball land
Softly, happy-safe
From my waiting overhead smash.

I wrote that poem the first week. Most of what I wrote the last week rhymed. We'd spent two whole days of class this week writing nothing but silly poems, kind of like what Shel Silverstein writes. That was the assignment. Mr. Gallagher said, "Some people think that silly poems are harder to write than serious ones, so here's my challenge: I want you to spend the next two days writing only silly poems. If you can try ten different poem ideas and two of them are good, you're ahead of the game."

I was glad he gave us that assignment. If I wrote what I was really feeling, I'd end up with poems too depressing to read, or else poems so personal I wouldn't dare read them.

None of my silly poems are anywhere near as good as Silverstein's, but I picked out three of them to read anyway, mostly because Mr. Gallagher said he liked them. He said I have a good ear for rhythm. I don't know if that's true, but it made me feel good when he said it.

When I read, I know I read faster than I should. It's just that I'm nervous and want to finish as soon as possible.

Baking Watermelon

I baked a watermelon cake
    With green rind and black seeds.
I used some sand for icing,
    For candles I used weeds.

It tasted far too gritty,
    And, sad to say, too dry.
I guess next time I'll try to bake
    A watermelon pie.

Friday Is My Day

Friday is my day to do what I like,
And what I like best is to ride on my bike,
To ride across recess, to ride down the hall,
To ride in my classroom and laugh at them all.

They are sitting there working for teachers who yell
From the morning announcementstil the day's final bell.
My classmates just sit there, all writing a poem,
So I zoom out the door and I ride my bike home.

Sally, Eating a Bar of Chocolate in Sunday School

The chocolate bar she tried to eat
Had melted in the summer heat.
The chocolate dripped off Sally's nose
And landed on her best church clothes.
Sally's favorite yellow dress
Was now a brown and gooey mess.
Some chocolate fell with a kerplop
And formed a heart-shaped chocolate drop
On one of Sally's new, white shoes.
The moral's this: if you should choose
To ever eat a chocolate bar,
Remember when and where you are.

I actually wrote that last one for Allison, but I changed her name because Mr. Gallagher said we shouldn't use the names of real people in our poems, because it might embarrass them or make them feel bad (even though the poem isn't true). It could have happened, though. Allison actually was eating a candy bar one day before Sunday School. She had on a really pretty dress. I kept thinking, "I hope she's careful not to get chocolate on her dress." She didn't, but she could have.

Mr. Gallagher told us more than once, "Poems

aren't always 'what is.' Most of the time they're
'what might be,' or 'what could be.'"

Allison's the last one in our class to read. I love
her poems. I think they say a lot about the kind of
person she is. Whether she's writing serious poems
or silly ones, most of them are about God or Jesus or
church or prayer.

She starts out with "God, Sticking Up For My
Brother."

I saw God sitting in a tree.
"It's only an owl," my brother said.
"Just listen to the sound."

It sure sounded like God to me.

Then in the middle of the night
I awoke to see God
in the shadows near my window.

"Why," I asked Him, "aren't you
still in the tree where I saw you
when I was in the yard with my brother?"

"I wasn't in that tree," God told me.
"That was an owl. Even brothers,"
God said, "are not wrong all the time."

Her next one is "Samson." Allison sure knows more about the Bible than I do.

Talk about being hoodwinked! He never did
see the truth until that final moment, chained
like a wild animal to be spit on by Philistines.
God could have given up on him; no one
would have blamed Him, gullible and ungodly
as Samson was, murderer of thirty men at Ashkelon,
of a thousand at Lehi. The woman of Timnath and
Delilah both saw the human Samson, Samson the weak.
But Samson, at the end, learned in time that prayer,
not hair, was the source of miraculous strength.

Allison reads one of her silly poems next. And it has nothing to do with religion.

A Cuddly Pet

Mom asked what I wanted for Christmas. She said,
"I'll try as hard as I can to get it.

I told her that pandas are furry and cuddly
And I'd like to have one so I can pet it.

There were none to be found, so Mom brought me home
A substitute pet, and she warned, "Don't upset it."

The pet that she brought me, a fat porcupine,
Was all right, I guess. But cuddle? Forget it.

"My last poem," Allison says, "is one titled 'A Child Knows God.'" She smiles out at the audience. She doesn't seem nervous or self-conscious at all. She says, "I thought back to when I was real little and first discovered how good God is. I didn't know anything about poetry then, but I think this is what I would have written if I had. It's exactly how I felt. It's how I still feel."

She starts to read.

God made the grass; God made each tree.
God gave me eyes so I can see
The grass he made and see the shade
That comforts me.

The way her face glows lets everyone know how much she loves God. She's not pretending, the way some people do. I wish I could feel the way she does. I want to. I really do.

God made the night; God made the day.
At night I sleep so I can play
At morning's light and do what's right
In every way.

God gave us life; he made us all.
And even though he made me small,

His love for me will help me be
So big and tall.

I know that God will help me grow
And learn all that I need to know
Of his kind deeds. He'll fill my needs.
I love him so!

When she finishes everybody claps hard. She hadn't seemed self-conscious before, but now she looks likes she's embarrassed. I think it's because of all the clapping.

She looks over at me. I wait for the clapping to stop. Then I walk out to the microphone and stand beside her. We're going to read a poem we wrote together, and that will end our class's part of the program. By together I mean we'll read alternate stanzas. The poem is the one we wrote in class about the months. We ended up spending a lot of time on it. It went through a ton of revisions, but I think it turned out pretty good. Allison wrote most of the best lines.

We wrote it in a series of couplets. A couplet is a two-line stanza. We've practiced reading it a lot. We decided that Allison will read the first couplet and I'll read the second one. We'll just keep alternating.

"This last poem," Allison says, "is one Kate Adams and I wrote together. It's called 'Parade of Months.'"

January skimmed on skates and did a figure eight.
February sloshed on boots; he didn't hesitate.

I'm nervous, but as soon as Allison finishes reading "hesitate," I read:

Arm and arm with Abe and George he rushed a Valentine
To March, who gave him in return a ray of spring sunshine.

We read the rest of the poem and don't mess up once:

Sweet April walked ahead of them, white blossoms in her hair.
She carried baseball bats and gloves through breezes oh so fair.

A long way in the distance she saw May, who was no fool.
For May was sprinting far ahead to reach the end of school.

Perhaps the most distracted in the parade was June.
Her thoughts were full of weddings and of summer, coming soon.

July's straw hat, wide-brimmed and orange, received its share of smirks
Before it got knocked off amidst a blast of fireworks.

valley lakes program

Poor August was so hot he sat and rested in the shade.
If somehow he could change with March he'd surely make the trade.

September marched triumphantly to school bells loud and clear.
She wore the lovely, fragrant smell of autumn growing near.

Some golden leaves blew on the path where crisp October strode.
With black cats, ghosts, and skeletons he headed up the road.

November had to wear a coat because of cooling weather
As it and friends and family all gathered close together.

December led the big parade with robust Christmas cheer,
And saw ahead a new parade of still another year.

As soon as we finish, everybody cheers. We even get a couple of loud whistles. I'm sure one of the whistlers is Ken.

Our class goes to a room offstage until the program is over, so we don't get to see the other two classes perform, instrumental music and drama. I don't really mind, though, because we got to see them all in rehearsals yesterday and today.

Ginny's class isn't doing anything from *Romeo and Juliet*. Instead they're acting out scenes from three different plays.

The scenes were chosen so that each of the students has about the same amount of time on stage to act their part. In Ginny's scene she plays an old lady. She's made up to look old, and she does a great job with her voice. She sounds like she's about ninety. She's not the only good one, though. Just about everybody on stage does a great job. It makes me glad I was chosen for creative writing. I could never in a million years be an actress.

We have a final curtain call, when everybody goes on stage. As soon as the curtain call is over, I run down to find Mama and Dad and Ken.

Dad hugs me first, but Mama's not far behind. "I'm so proud of you, Kate," she says. "Your poems were wonderful."

"I didn't know you could write that well," Dad says. "You never cease to amaze me."

Ken taps my shoulder and says, "My favorite poem was the one Allison read about the owl. I loved that line about brothers not being wrong."

"If she knew you better," I say, "she never would have written it."

"Ha ha," Ken says.

I'd been ready to quit the school after I found out about Mama's cancer. I'm really glad I stuck it out. The last week especially was fun. And I know if I hadn't been coming to school I would have spent every minute worrying about Mama.

But there's one good thing about school being over. Mama quit her job this week. Now I'll be able to be with her all the time.

eighteen

tennis match

Last week's Fourth of July fireworks display was spectacular. It must have lasted for half an hour with one exploding shower of color after another. I didn't enjoy it much, though. Every explosion and every stream of colors sprinkling from the sky to the ground made me think of things dying. I'd never thought about it before, not in all the years I'd been watching fireworks and feeling all tingly at how pretty I thought they were.

Mama was right beside me and oohing and aahing like she does every Fourth of July. I keep looking for signs that she's getting better. Mostly, though, I keep hoping I don't see signs she's getting worse. If I don't see them that might mean the doctors are wrong and she'll be all right after all.

In the two weeks since Valley Lakes School ended, I haven't left home much. There's no place I want to go. I just want to spend time with Mama. She seems the same as always, always busy doing something. She doesn't seem sick, not really. I notice that she takes more breaks from whatever she's doing than she usually does. Like when she works in her garden. She would spend hours without stopping except to get a drink of water or something like that. Now she's starting to get tired sooner. She'll go and sit down, or maybe go inside and not go back to the garden at all for the rest of the day.

Today's been a good day, though. The way Mama is playing tennis today makes me think that she's not sick after all. The two of us are beating Dad and Ken. It's not like they're letting us win. I can tell. We're just hitting better shots than they are.

There've been a few balls that Mama usually returns for winners that have caught the top of the net, but I'm thinking that's only because she's rusty. She hasn't played much the last few weeks. Even so, we won the first set 6–4 and we lead in the second set 4 games to 2. Mom is serving at 40–15.

I have to admit, I'm playing as good as I ever have. I'm not going to let us lose today, no matter what.

Just beyond the end line on the other side of the net, Ken is bouncing on the balls of his feet, balanced, waiting for Mama's serve.

"We need this point, partner," Dad calls over his shoulder to Ken.

"No way," I shout.

The ball whizzes past my right ear and lands well in service court. Ken lunges across his body, and the ball pings off the center of his racket. He doesn't hit it deep. It'll come down in the middle of our court, perfect for a winning return.

I move back toward the ball just as Mama moves forward. We've been partners long enough that I know she'll back off and let me take it. The overhead smash is my best shot. I win a lot of points with it.

I race to where the ball will bounce so I'll be ready. I see Mama still coming toward the ball as if she plans to hit it.

"Mine!" I call out and Mama backs away.

I swing.

I can't believe it. Either there's a gust of wind or else I take my eye off the ball for an instant. But instead of hitting a sure winner, the ball hits the top edge of my racquet and goes straight up about twenty feet, then almost hits me on the way down.

Ken drops his racquet and falls to the court, laughing. He lies on his back and kicks his legs in the air. He bounces up and imitates my overhead swing. He holds his sides and laughs harder.

"Son," Dad says. He sees I'm laughing too and

just shakes his head.

"No problem," I say. "We're still up 40–30. Sorry, Mama."

Suddenly Dad is running toward our side of the court. I look back and see Mama sitting down. I know I didn't hit her with my racquet, I would have felt it.

"Are you okay, honey?" Dad asks.

"Just feeling a little dizzy," Mama says. "I'll be okay in a minute."

"I think we've had enough for today," Dad says. "Sixteen games, and it's pretty hot this afternoon."

"Just give me a minute," Mama says. "We'll be able to finish the set."

She walks to the bench and takes a drink of water. She sits down and towels herself off.

"We don't have to finish," Dad says.

"We'll finish this set," Mama says firmly.

Mama serves at 40–30, a good serve, and Dad's return goes wide. We lead 5 games to 2.

As we switch sides of the court, I see Dad talking softly to Ken.

It's Dad's serve. It's not his best serve, and I hit a hard baseline winner. "Love-fifteen," he calls out. "Okay, Ken, let's get this point."

Serving toward Mama's court, he double faults. He hardly ever double faults.

Mama glares at him, her hands on her hips. "Just

play the game," she calls out.

He serves to me, and Ken hits my return into the net. It's Love–40. Match point.

I think I know what will happen next, but I hope it doesn't.

It does. Another double fault. The match is over.

Mama doesn't even look at Dad. She just grabs her drink and towel and tennis bag and heads for the car. Mama and Dad hardly ever argue or even get mad at each other, but there's sure plenty of anger in her eyes right now.

nineteen

dad knew

After the tennis match last week, Mama and Dad both kept trying to out-apologize the other.

"I'm sorry," Dad said.

"No," Mama said. "I'm sorry. I overreacted. I know you were just worried about me."

"I was," Dad said. "But I should have known you were strong enough to finish the set."

"I should have known I wasn't," Mama said.

And so on and so forth.

I know now it was an important day. I have to write about it. I have to try, anyway. The blank page of my notebook stares back at me. If it could talk it would probably say, "I dare you to write a poem. I bet you can't."

The trouble is, it's right.

I try to remember some of the things that Mr. Gallagher taught us. One thing I remember him saying is, "A poem, whether it's a story poem or picture poem, is simply an accumulation of details. You just start writing about the things you see, the things that happen, the way you feel. Just let one thought lead into another, just the way you think them." So I take my pen and just let the thoughts come.

Dad was right.

Mama was wrong. I'm sorry, Mama, but you were.

I wish with all my heart you weren't.

The cancer is making you sicker. Weaker.

When you think no one is looking

I see you bite your lip to try to hide your pain.

I watch you sit to rest, more often than you ever have.

I hear your laughter, treasure your every smile.

I know yours are real; I have to force mine.

I have to pretend I'm happy.

I know you're not giving up.

You've seen other doctors, gotten other opinions.

They all agree.

Chemo won't help.

Radiation treatments won't help.

dad knew

Surgery isn't an option.

Nothing is left except time. Time and hope.

It seems as if time has wings and is carrying

you away, Mama, far away,

and so fast I can't keep up.

I don't want you to leave my sight

but no matter how hard I try

I can't figure out how to stop time.

I can only hope it's flying toward a miracle.

I read over what I wrote. I don't tear the page out and throw it away like I have some other things I've tried to write.

I know, though, that I'm not going to show it to Mama.

twenty

friday night tradition

So much has changed this summer. At least our Friday nights have stayed the same. Mostly. Except on those nights when we go to a football game or a play or visit friends or something, we keep to our Friday night tradition: the four of us in the TV/game room, playing games or watching DVDs and eating popcorn and other snacks, our normal Friday night.

Normal is a strange word. I don't even know what normal is anymore.

That first Friday, right after I found out about Mama's cancer, I couldn't be with Mama and Dad. I just couldn't. But that was the only time I haven't been part of our tradition.

Mama and Dad must be picking out funny movies to watch on purpose. I'm glad. It helps me forget for a little while about the bad thing that's taking over our lives.

Last Friday something different happened. Just a few minutes before the end of the movie, Ken got up and started to leave the room. He didn't say anything.

Dad picked up the remote. He said, "I'll pause it until you come back." We all just figured he was going to the bathroom or something.

"That's okay," Ken said. "Keep it running. I have to go to my room. I'm not going to watch the rest."

"But it's almost over," Mama said.

Ken didn't answer. He just left. The three of us watched the rest of the movie without him.

The movie had a really cool ending. I wished Ken had stayed to see it. He would have liked it. I know he would have. I think Mama and Dad felt bad, too, that he didn't see it.

Tonight, same time as always, Mama gets out the popcorn popper. I'm not talking about those air poppers that throw out dry, tasteless popcorn, or even microwave popcorn which is sometimes tasteless but sometimes even pretty good if you buy the kind with gobs of butter melted into it. I'm talking about the old dented popcorn pan Mama always uses, with popcorn popped in just the right amount of vegetable oil and doused with just the right amount of melted butter with just the right amount of the special seasoned salt Mama sprinkles on it.

That's the kind of popcorn I get to look forward to almost every Friday night. That's the only night we have it. "We don't want to every get tired of it," Mama says every time I beg for it on any other night. "If we pop it more often we'll get tired of it. It won't be special anymore."

I always start pouting when she says that, but deep down I know she's right. That popcorn—not just the taste but the tradition—is one thing that makes our Friday night family time so special.

"It's almost time for the movie," Dad calls out while he gets the DVD ready. "Tell Ken."

"Ken. Hurry up!" I yell from the hallway. I wait a few seconds for him to come out of his room. He doesn't even answer.

"Ken!" I shout again.

Nothing.

I finally give up and go to the door of his room. His door is shut, so I knock. I've learned not to go in his room without knocking. Even last year I could go in without knocking, but now he gets really mad, like his privacy is the most precious thing in the whole world. Heaven forbid I should open his door and see him in his underwear or something. Like I've never seen his underwear before.

And I know he's not going to be in his room smoking or taking drugs or looking at naked girls on the Internet. Ken's my little brother. I know him. You can't be as close as we have for all that time to not know the things he does and doesn't do.

I knock louder.

"Come on in," he calls out. "It's not locked."

He's lying on his bed with his earphones on. I'm surprised he heard me at all, as loud as his music is playing. I can even hear it through his earphones, and I'm way across the room.

He takes them off.

"You'll be as deaf as a stone before you're in high school," I say.

"Like it matters," he says.

"Well, what about Grandma Chambers?" I say. She's not completely deaf, but she's close to it. We all have to shout really loud for her to hear anything we say. It's hard on her, but it's hard on us, too, because we can't really carry on a conversation with her. "Do you want to end up like her?"

"I'm not playing it that loud," he says.

I figure this isn't the best time to argue with him about his music. "It's time for the movie. Mama's doing popcorn and Dad has the movie all ready to go."

Ken shakes his head.

"What's that supposed to mean?"

"I can't watch it."

"It's Friday night. We all watch it. Mama and Dad are waiting. You can't disappoint Mama."

"I don't want to disappoint her. But I can't watch a movie. I can't even watch any television."

I start to ask why, but I suddenly realize I haven't seen him watching TV at all in the past week. The last time was when he walked out of the room before the movie was over a week ago.

"But you love movies," I say. "You love television."

"That was before," he says. "I can't watch anymore."

"Before what?"

"You know."

"Okay. Things are different," I say. "You don't think I know that?"

He just shrugs.

"Are you just going to stay here and make me go out and tell Mama you don't want to be with her?"

"Tell her I'm sick."

"But you're not," I say.

"I will be," he says, "if I go out there and somebody dies in whatever movie we'll be watching. Like they did in the last one."

Now I remember. It starts to make sense. Last week's movie had been a funny one, but there was a scene, just a little one, not important really, where a kid who was invited to a party couldn't go because his grandmother had just died. I mean, we hadn't even met his grandmother in the movie. It's not like it was any big, sad thing. I remember that Ken walked out right after that.

"Every time I watch something on TV," Ken says, "somebody dies. I never noticed before. I mean, I did, but it didn't seem to matter. A dozen guys could get shot in just one hour and I didn't care. Just so long as the story was exciting, that's all I cared about. But now I know it does matter. One second a person is breathing and has his whole life ahead of him. The next minute he isn't. It scares me too much. It's too sad."

"But ..." That's as far as I get because he interrupts.

"And I know it's going to happen. It's going to happen to Mama."

"Hurry up in there!" It's Dad, calling from the TV room.

"Okay!" I call back.

"How about this?" I say. "I'll go out and find out what we're going to watch. If it's something where nobody dies, will you watch? Mama needs you, now more than ever."

"I don't know if I can. What if I have to walk out in the middle of the movie? You can't be sure nobody will die."

"I know," I say. "But Mama's alive. Tonight she

is. That's all that's important now."

"I don't know if I can."

"For Mama," I say. "You have to."

Ken shakes his head. He takes a deep breath. Then he gets up from the bed and clicks off his music. He rubs the back of his hand across his eyes.

The thing is, I know how Ken feels. It's how my thoughts about the orphans in the play *Annie* changed after Mama got sick.

"It better be a funny movie," he says. "It had just better."

twenty-one

standing in the bleachers

Dad's been coming to all our baseball games.
Sometimes Mama's been too sick to come. They
argue about it. Not really argue. Disagree. Dad
always says he's going to stay home with her. She
needs him, he says. Mama always tells him to go
to the game. She says she'll be okay for a couple of
hours.

Mama always wins. I'm glad. I love for Dad to be
at our games. I just hate it that Mama can't come.

Mama's feeling better today, so she is at the game
with Dad. It rained this afternoon and it's cool this
evening. Not cold enough for a jacket or anything, a
perfect temperature to play baseball. Except Mama's
wearing a jacket. She's the only one I see wearing one.

It makes me sad to see it. It's like proof—as if I didn't already know—that she's getting more and more sick all the time. I've seen Mama playing tennis in short sleeves and shorts when the temperature is in the forties. Cold has never seemed to bother her. Until now.

I don't want anybody to think I've spent the whole game watching Mama and worrying about her. The game is one of the most exciting we've played all summer, except for that first one, of course. I don't think I'll ever play in a baseball game that will be more exciting than that one. I don't suppose I'll ever make another game-winning hit. But in this one we're tied in the sixth inning. If the game goes extra innings, I might have a chance to bat again, but I hope it doesn't. I hope we score the winning run right now.

I made an out in the fifth inning, so there's no way I can possibly come up to bat this inning. We have our number nine hitter Toby leading off in the sixth, then our leadoff hitter Jake, our number two hitter Ken, and if somebody gets on, our best hitter. That's Ivy.

I'm batting seventh in the order. So I figured out that before it can be my turn to hit we'll either have three outs this inning or else we'll have scored the winning run.

Toby has only two hits all year, and the guy

throwing for the other team is the fastest guy we've faced this season. We're lucky to be tied. They've got about nine or ten hits, and we only have two, but we're tied three to three. We've made some great catches. They could have scored a lot more. We were lucky to score at all. In the fourth inning their pitcher struck out our first two batters, then he walked Jake and Ken singled. Ivy hit a fly ball to right field that should have been an easy out, but the right fielder dropped the ball. Both runners scored and Ivy got all the way to second base. The next batter, Andy, hit a fly ball to right and he dropped this one too. Ivy scored our third run.

Then an awful thing happened.

Their coach ran half way to right field and waved at the right fielder to come in off the field. He sent somebody else out to take his place. Right in the middle of the inning. I shouldn't have been sur-prised. It was the same coach I saw pull his shortstop off the field in the middle of an inning during one of Ken's games last year.

The poor kid that dropped those two fly balls was crying when he got to the bench. He sat down on the end of the bench and covered his head with a towel. I know he was still crying. He probably didn't want anybody to see him. A couple of his teammates came over and patted him on the shoulder. It looked like they were maybe trying to make him feel better.

He just pushed them away, though.

It wouldn't surprise me if the poor kid never played baseball again.

"That's all right, Toby!" Coach calls out. Toby's walking back to the bench with his head down. He just struck out. The pitcher is just too fast for him. Toby never had a chance, but he at least went down swinging.

If we can get Jake on, we've got a chance with Ken and Ivy coming up. Jake's the perfect lead-off batter. He's the shortest guy on our team, and he doesn't strike out much. He fouls off a lot of pitches, and the more pitches a pitcher throws, the more chance there is he'll walk Jake, which happens a lot.

But not this time. Jake hits a pop-up that their first baseman doesn't hardly even have to move for.

Ken has one of our two hits, and he really needs one now. If he can just get on, Ivy can win it for us.

Ken swings and I jump to my feet. So does everybody else on our bench. I can't believe it! He's just hit maybe the longest ball he's hit all year, way out in right field. It clears the fence by about ten feet. I see him stop halfway to first base. I don't know why. He turns and comes back to home plate.

The umpire called it foul.

I didn't have a good look at it, but the ump must have got the call right. Nobody argues.

"Nice swing, Ken!" Coach calls out. "Just missed

it by a couple feet."

I look back at the bleachers. Everybody is on their feet. Even Mama. She has a big smile on her face, and I guess she's not cold after all, because her jacket is off now.

"Do it again, Ken!" she shouts. "You can do it!"

And he does!

I'm not saying it's because of what Mama said. That's too spooky. But on his next swing, he hits it almost the same place, but this one clears the right field fence just inside the foul line.

We all rush out on the field toward Ken. On my way I glance toward the bleachers. Mama is grinning and yelling and hugging Dad. She reminds me of a little kid on Christmas morning. Her cheeks aren't their usual pale white; they're rosy. Her eyes are bright. She looks like she hasn't been sick a day in her life.

twenty-two

never blame the umpire

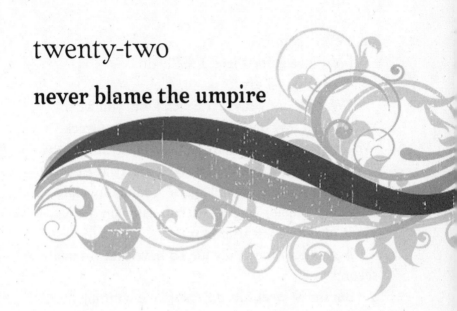

"We're going to Adventure Land Amusement Park next week!" Ginny squeals over the phone. "My parents just said you can come, too. We'll have a super time!"

Adventure Land Amusement Park! It's one of my favorite places. And not just because of the neat rides. A part of the park is like a combination jungle-zoo with a bunch of wild animals. You get on a train and ride right past them, almost close enough to touch them. And there's lots of other fun things to do. I've been to Disney World, and Adventure Land is almost as great. What makes Adventure Land even better for me is that it's only four hours away, close enough that I usually get to go there at least once every summer.

I just love going there. I really do.

"I can't go," I say.

"Wait," Ginny says. "I haven't told you when we're going. My dad gets his vacation next week. We'll be going on Tuesday, and we'll stay in a motel Tuesday night, spend all day Wednesday at Adventure Land, stay at a motel again Wednesday night, and go to a major league baseball game on the way home on Thursday afternoon."

Any other time in my life I'd have said yes in a second.

But in the week since Ken's game-winning home run Mama's gotten a lot worse. She hardly eats anything. When she does try to eat, she usually ends up in the bathroom throwing up. It seems like she's getting thinner and weaker every day. She hasn't even tried to play tennis since that match right after the Fourth of July when she got tired and quit early and got mad at Dad. I just can't be away from Mama now. Not for three whole days.

"It sounds fun. I wish I could go. But this isn't a good time. Don't you have play rehearsal anyway?"

"I'll just miss two rehearsals. And my dad had me talk to the director before he made vacation plans. Our director told me which nights they'll be working on scenes I'm not going to be in. She said it's okay if I miss those two rehearsals."

I feel bad about not being able to go, but I feel worse about letting Ginny down. "Well, maybe you can ask Allison or Ivy to go with you."

"I know why you want to stay home, but I think you should go. It's only for a couple days."

A couple of days. Three, actually. Anything can happen in three days.

"I know. But I can't go. Really. I just can't."

"Go where?" Mama is standing in the doorway. I don't know how long she's been there or how much she's heard.

I hold my hand over the phone. "It's Ginny. She's asked me to go with them to Adventure Land next week."

"You told her you can't?"

I nod.

Mama takes my phone from me. "Hi, Ginny," she says. "Kate will call you right back." She closes it and hands it to me.

"Now," she says. "You love Adventure Land. Why aren't you going?"

"It's going to be for three whole days. They're leaving Tuesday and not coming back until Thursday night."

"So? What big plans do you have for next week?"

What I'm thinking is, "I don't want to leave you," but what I say is, "We have our last ballgame on Friday."

"So? You'll be back in plenty of time."

"I'll miss practice."

"I don't think your coach will mind. You've been at practically every practice all summer."

"But I'll be gone three days."

Mama takes my arm and sits on the sofa, pulling me down beside her. "Kate. Sweetheart. It's been a hard summer for you, for all of us. But it's been a fun summer, too, hasn't it? I've had such a good time being able to spend so much of it with you and Ken and your father. But you need time with your friends, too. I think you need to go."

"I can't." Does she really think I would leave her for all that time?

"I want you to. I know you worry about me, but I'll be fine while you're gone." She gives me one of her big smiles. "You know that your father will take good care of me."

"I know, Mama. But ... three days."

"I want you to have this special time with Ginny. It will mean a lot to me."

I study Mama's face. I try to read something into it that will tell me if she means it or if she's just pretending. I can't be certain. "Are you sure?" I ask.

"Yes, I am." She pulls me close and gives me a big hug.

"We can't just sit around expecting the worst," she says. "We have to make the most of every day.

And this is the time for you to enjoy Adventure Land with Ginny and her family. I'll miss you while you're gone, but it will make me very happy knowing you're having a good time with your best friend."

"I just don't know..."

"You must go," she says. "For me." She stands and walks over to the bookcase. She picks up a photo Dad took of Ken and me in our baseball uniforms. "I've watched you and Ken play baseball this summer, and I've been so proud of you. Not just because of how well you've both played and how hard you've worked to improve, but because you've had fun playing. And you know something else? I've thought a lot about the umpires."

"The umpires?"

Her eyes are bright. They seem alive. I can't understand how she can be so sick and her eyes look so alive. "Umpires," she says. "You need them to control the game. Of course, the players and coaches and fans don't always agree with the umpire's calls. Sometimes we get mad at them and wonder how they could have made the calls they did."

"That's for sure," I say. "Like the game against Logansville, when they called their runner safe at first in the last inning. The game should have been over. Then their next batter hit a home run to beat us. If they'd made the right call, we would have won the game." Just thinking about that moment again makes me mad. Even the Logansville players were joking after the game about how the ump missed that call. I still don't know how the ump was the only person in the ballpark who couldn't see the player was out by at least a full step.

"I remember that play. That was a shame. But when you think about it, God and umpires have a lot in common."

"God and umpires?" I've been going to Sunday School my whole life, but I've never heard anybody compare God to a baseball umpire before.

"Just think about it. Think about all the decisions an umpire has to make during a baseball game. Is it a ball or strike? Is the runner out or safe?" Mama walks to a shelf and picks up the scorecard that Ken had filled out the last time we went to a Kansas City Royals game. "Remember this game? We went to see the players, but the umpires were important. The players and the fans too have to trust that the umpires will make the right call. They can't just quit if they don't like the umpire's call. We can't quit if we don't like God's decision." Mama sets the scorecard back down and takes my hand. She squeezes it. I love the touch of her hand on mine. She says, "Of course, God doesn't make mistakes like umpires sometimes do."

"How can you say that?" I pull away from her. I don't mean to. It's like when you touch a hot pan.

You can't help but pull your hand away. It's as if Mama's words have burned me. God did make a mistake. A terrible one. "God made a mistake by letting you get sick. If God ..." I can't finish my thought. Not out loud. I can't speak the words I'm thinking, that if God lets Mama die, he's making the most terrible mistake anybody can make.

"I know how you feel, honey," Mama says softly. "But let me finish. Just listen. I want you to see that umpires are human, and humans make mistakes. God doesn't. God has a plan. We might not understand it, but it doesn't mean he is wrong, or that he's made a mistake. We get mad at God sometimes, just like we get mad at umpires. We think that God is wrong sometimes. We wonder how he could have made such a terrible decision. We blame God for the bad things, just as we blame umpires for the bad things in ball games."

I shake my head back and forth. I still don't understand. "But it's like you said, God isn't human. So I don't understand how he can let bad things happen."

"That's the mystery of God," Mama says. "We can't see the future, so maybe what we think is bad might really be something God lets happen so that something even worse won't happen in the future."

"I don't believe that."

"Think about it. Isn't it possible? That's another one of God's mysteries that we humans can never know. And remember this, too, about umpires. No matter how we feel about an umpire's decision, we have to accept it. The umpire is the authority in every ball game. If we challenge the umpire's authority too strongly, we might end up having to forfeit the game. God is the ultimate authority in our lives." Mama takes my hand again. This time I don't pull away. I want to feel her touch. I never want to lose the feeling of her hand in mine.

"We might not agree with his every decision," Mama says, "we may not even understand it—but we need to accept it. If we reject his authority and challenge his decisions, we might ultimately have to forfeit all that he has offered us. Our life is like a ball game, and I am winning, no matter what happens, because I'm trying to play by God's rules. I accept his will for me."

I've never thought about umpires being like God. It sure doesn't seem fair to God to compare him to an umpire. I've been so mad at God that I have this terrible thought that maybe it's not fair to the umpire. I feel guilty thinking that. I try to pretend I never thought it.

I can see that some of what Mama says makes sense.

"I love you, Mama," I cry, burying my head on her shoulder. "I love you so much."

"I love you, darling," Mama whispers.

"What you just said, about God and umpires.

I've never thought about it like that."

"There's one more thing I want you to remember," Mama says. "There is one big difference, the most important difference of all. We need God in our lives far more than a game needs an umpire. God didn't give me my cancer. We mustn't blame him. God is helping me deal with any pain and sadness the cancer has caused." She gives my hand a squeeze.

"Now call Ginny," she says.

So I do.

twenty-three

adventure land

Adventure Land was so much fun I bet I went an hour or two at a time without thinking of Mama. Of course, then I felt guilty when I remembered her at home, sick and in pain.

Now Ginny and I are out by the swimming pool at the motel where we're going to stay tonight. For the first half hour or so Ginny and I had the pool all to ourselves. We could dive and have races without worrying about other people getting in our way.

Then a bunch of other people jumped into the pool, so Ginny and I got out and sprawled out on deck chairs. Ginny brought along a book to read, and I have my journal with me.

I've been writing in my journal almost every

day since Mr. Gallagher's class. He told us that
most writers, and people who want to be writers,
keep daily journals to help them remember ideas
that might become stories and poems. He said
that writing every day and keeping journals helps
a writer develop a personal style. He told us that
the best advice he ever got was that if he wanted
to be a writer he must first write a million words.
After someone writes a million words they start to
develop a personal style.

A million words. He must have been kidding. I'm
pretty sure that's more than I'll ever be able to write.
But who knows. If I can write a few hundred words
a week they'll start to add up.

Another thing Mr. Gallagher said is that keeping
a journal can be like therapy. It can help a person
sort through all their confusing feelings.

I've had a lot of them this summer.

Now that I've gotten in the habit of keeping a
journal, I can't imagine not keeping one. I know
there won't probably be a lot of time to write when
Ginny and I get back to our room, so I decide to
write now, while Ginny is reading her book.

Something I've been trying to do lately is try to
write my journal entries as poems. At least I'm trying
to make them look like poems. Most of the time I
don't even plan what I'm going to write. I just let the
thoughts come.

adventure land

I had fun today.
I didn't realize that having fun
Could make a person feel bad.
I don't have the right to have fun
When Mama is so sick.
I've phoned her a few times every day.
She always tells me that she hopes
I'm having a good time.
"I am, Mama," I tell her.
When I hang up, I feel guilty
That I didn't even have to lie to her.
I guess I'd feel guilty no matter what
Because I should be home with her
Even though I'm glad I'm here.
You'd say I'm being silly, wouldn't you, Mama,
Even though I don't feel at all silly.
Her pain seems to be worse.
I can see it in her face. I can see it
In the way she turns away to hide her pain from me.
Even the pain medication Dad gives her
Doesn't seem to help.
I think maybe Mama wanted me to come with Ginny
Not just because it would be fun for me.

I think another reason was so
She wouldn't have to work so hard
To hide her pain from me these past three days.
I'm sorry, Mama, for having such a good time.

I close my notebook. It's a beautiful day. The water in the pool is the perfect temperature. I don't want to be sad anymore. Not today. I know Mama wouldn't want me to be sad.

"Want to swim some more?" I ask Ginny.

"Sure," she says. "Just let me finish this chapter. I'm in a really exciting part."

I open my notebook again. I want to write about something happy. The first thing that pops into my head is the two boys we met yesterday.

Waiting in line for the Monster Coaster ride.
Ginny and me.
Giggling and not paying attention
To anyone around us until someone says,
"You have a nice giggle."
There were two boys right behind us.
Two cute boys. Our age, I think.
Maybe a year older.
I don't know if it was Ginny or me
Who he thought had a nice giggle.

We talked to them for the ten minutes or so
We stood in line for our ride.
We found out they live about six hours from us.
We found out they love baseball.
Ginny told them that we do too. A white lie
(about her loving baseball). She glared at me
so I knew enough to not tell them the truth.
They sat right behind us on the Monster Coaster.
But we didn't even get their names.
And they didn't get ours.
After we all left the Monster Coaster
We never saw them again.

Somebody just jumped from the diving board
and made a splash so big a few drops of water land
on my journal. I look up. I can't believe it. One of the
boys in the pool looks like one of the guys I've been
writing about from the Monster Coaster.

"Ginny!" I whisper.

But then I take a closer look and see it's not him
after all.

For a second there I thought I might have a more
interesting poem to write.

I remember Mr. Gallagher telling us we can
change reality when we write a poem. We don't have
to stick to the truth.

I think about how I can change my poem. I can pretend they got our names and email addresses and promised to write. I can even write about how they ended up moving to our town and going to the same school. About how we ended up dating them in high school and going to the prom with them.

You can do anything you want in a poem.

twenty-four

the umpire's call

When I got home last night, Ken said our team had its best practice of the summer. He thinks it's because I wasn't there. He was just joking, though. I think.

I asked him about Mama, and he said she didn't seem to be hurting as much.

I'm glad she feels well enough to come to our game today.

It's the last inning. At least it should be. We're ahead 9–3, so unless we fall apart in the last of the sixth and give up enough runs for the Tigers to tie the score, it will be our final inning.

The best thing about playing baseball this summer is that Mama and Dad have come to a lot of our

games. They missed one other when Mama had a
real bad spell and almost had to go to the hospital.

Ginny's even come to a few of my games.

The bad thing about summer baseball is that I
used up all my hero time in that first game.

I'm not the worst hitter on the team, but I'm only
average. Okay, maybe not even as good as average.
I've gotten a few hits this summer, just none that
have won games for us since that first one. My field-
ing is the best part of my game. I think that's because
I've played so much tennis. I have quick hands and
strong wrists and good hand-eye coordination. I have
strong legs, too, so I can move quick. I can catch the
ball most of the time, and I can throw pretty hard.
I know those things that make me a good fielder
should make me a better hitter, too. It's just that it's
easier for me to hit a tennis ball with a big racquet
than it is to hit a baseball with that skinny bat.

Ken, on the other hand, is a great hitter. Even
though he's one of the youngest players on the team,
he's one of the team's three best hitters. I'm glad,
because Mama and Dad really get excited when he
comes to bat and gets a hit. And he gets a bunch of
them.

We have runners on second and third and one
out, so unless there's a double play I'll get one more
at-bat. I'd love to finish the season with a good hit. It
would be nice to score a couple more runs, too, just

in case the Tigers rally in their half. Like Coach says, no lead is ever too big. Baseball isn't like basketball or football or soccer, where you can run out of time. A baseball game is never over until you get the other team to make that final out.

The batter ahead of me doesn't hit into a double play, but we still have runners on second and third, and now there are two outs. I can drive in two runs with a base hit.

I'm hoping the pitcher will throw me one waist high, right across the plate. That's the pitch I can hit best. But the pitch is at my knees and I take it for a strike. He throws two high pitches and the ump calls them balls.

The next pitch is right where I want it, but I hit under it and foul it back into the screen. I don't want to strike out, so I'm ready to swing at anything close.

It's not close. It's about two feet over my head. Somehow the catcher catches it, so our runner has to stay at third. The count is three and two. I wouldn't mind walking. Reaching base in my last at-bat would be almost as good as getting a hit. People always say, "A walk is as good as hit." Ken doesn't believe it. He always says, "I don't want to walk, I want to swing the bat."

But I'm not that good a hitter. I'll be happy with a walk.

The pitcher throws the ball so low the ball bounces

on the plate. I toss down my bat and start toward
first base. I take about three steps before I hear the
ump yell, "Strike three! You're out!" I look back. The
catcher is holding the ball. It must have bounced right
into his mitt.

I stare at the ump. How could he call it a strike?
It hit the plate! Then I think, their catcher is a big
guy, about as wide as he is tall, maybe the ump got
blocked out and he didn't see it hit the plate.

There's a lot of shouting from the bleachers and
from our dugout. "It hit the plate, ump!" and "Get
some help from the base umpire!"

The ump must have heard them, but he just
bends down and brushes the dirt off home plate with
a little broom. It's bad enough to strike out in my last
at-bat, but to strike out because the umpire made one
of the most terrible calls I've ever seen … that's just
not fair.

I have to walk past him to get to the dugout.
I'm trying to figure out what to say to him. Then I
remember Mama is watching from the bleachers. I
glance toward her. Dad is shouting something, but
Mama's just sitting there, smiling. I wonder why
she's smiling. What happened isn't funny.

Suddenly I remember what Mama told me about
umpires. I glance toward the umpire and think,
"You're not God. You make mistakes, and you sure
made a whopper this time. But you're the authority. I

might not agree with you, but I'll accept your judgment."

I don't say those words out loud, but just thinking them makes me feel a little better. I look back at Mama. She's still smiling, and I see her give a little nod of her head. I know just what she's thinking. I smile back at her because we have our special secret.

twenty-five

the play

About a week after our last baseball game
Mama's pain got so bad that Dad had to take her
to the hospital. She stayed for almost ten days.
While she was there, each day seemed like it was a
hundred hours long. And each day seemed as if it
lasted for only a few minutes.

Maybe that doesn't make sense, but it really does,
to me anyway.

The liquid medicine she was hooked up with the
tubing in her arm helped with her pain, but it also
made her sleep most of the time. When she was
awake, it was hard to talk to her because it seemed
like what we were saying didn't make sense to her,
or else what she said was hard for us to understand.

I'd sit by her bed for hours, just hoping she might wake up long enough for me to talk to her. I'd pray she would be able to hear me and maybe even say something that let me know she understood me.

What made the days seem short is when I measured them by how much time I really had with her. That time went too fast.

Then, two days ago, it was almost like a miracle. Mama's terrible pain seemed to go away. Not completely, but enough so she seemed almost like herself again, like she was before she had to go to the hospital. Maybe it was her pain medication. Maybe God had decided she deserved a few days without that hurt. Whatever it was, it was like I finally had my mama back again. She could speak. She could understand. And maybe the best thing of all, she smiled again.

It wasn't the miracle I had prayed for, though. Mama is still going to die. She might have only a few weeks left, maybe only a few days.

We had three choices: keep Mama in the hospital, bring her home, or take her to a hospice. A hospice is a place where dying people can go to be treated. The workers there are trained to care for people who are dying. That means that the patient gets more care than they get in a hospital. From what I understand, at a hospice the workers help the patient face the fact that they're going to die and maybe not be so afraid.

"I want to come home," Mama said. "I want to spend what time I have in my own home with my family. You're what I need most. I want to look out at my garden. I want to be surrounded by my own furniture and the pictures on my walls. I want to see the books I've loved to read. I want to be in the house where my two children have grown up."

So Mama's home now. Unless her pain gets so bad she needs to go back to the hospital, Dad can take care of her. We can all take care of her.

"It might be only days," the doctor said. "Just try to keep her comfortable."

One thing Mama's talked about ever since Ginny got chosen to play Annie is how much she wants to see the play. But the play's still a few weeks away.

I talked to Ginny yesterday. I asked her if she would do something. I asked her if she would talk to the play's director for the biggest favor I've ever asked, except for the one I asked of God. Ginny called last night after rehearsal with the good news. "She said yes. You can come to our rehearsal tomorrow night. Your whole family." Before I'd talked to Ginny about my plan, I asked Dad what he thought. Did he think it would be too much for Mama?

He said, "Oh Kate, that's a wonderful idea. I can't think of anything she'd like better."

I pray that Mama feels good enough to go.

We make sure we don't tire her out during the
day by doing a lot of talking or making her talk. We
make sure she gets plenty of rest.

When it's time, Dad helps dress Mama and puts
her in her wheelchair. She's so thin. Her face is pale.
But she's beaming, and her green eyes are twinkling.

It's less than a ten-minute drive to the theater.
We've arranged to get there about half an hour after
the rehearsal started. Ginny said that would be best.
She said that at most rehearsals the first few minutes
are spent just taking care of loose ends from the pre-
vious rehearsal and setting up the scenes they'll be
working on that night.

They don't do the whole play. They only work
on a couple scenes, going over and over them, working on every little detail. Like where each character
should be on stage, even if that character isn't talking. And what each character should be doing. It
surprises me. I didn't know how much planning was
necessary. I guess I figured that all the characters
had to do is memorize their lines and get up and say
them.

The best thing: the scenes they rehearsed were
a couple of Annie's big scenes. So Mama gets to see
Ginny on stage practically the whole time. And she
gets to watch and listen to Ginny sing.

I've never seen Ginny better. It's like she's singing just to Mama. I know Mama has to be tired, but

the play

she stays awake through the whole rehearsal. It's
only when we get her in the car that she finally lets
herself fall asleep.

twenty-six

opening the bible

One of Mama's favorite things is to hear Ken and Dad and me read to her from the Bible. Her Bible is full of color where she's highlighted her favorite verses. One of them is John 4:27: "I am leaving you with a gift—peace of mind and heart! And the peace I give isn't fragile like the peace the world gives. So don't be troubled or afraid."

Another is Romans 12:12: "Be glad for all God is planning for you. Be patient in trouble, and prayerful always."

The first time I heard that verse I asked her, "How can you be glad? How can any of us be glad for bad things?"

She said, "Things only seem bad because we're

taught to look from the world's viewpoint. God's plan for us goes far beyond the time we have on earth."

Mama's sleeping now, in her own bed, in her own house. We've moved Mama's bed close to her window so she can look outside onto our big back yard and her flower and vegetable gardens. Today she feels good enough to ask us to read to her not just from the Bible but from the morning newspaper. "Read me some good news," she said. "Some fun things."

It seems like most of the news is bad.

But we read about a big tennis tournament that just ended. We read about some big league baseball games and about some players who did some special things. We tell her the Royals have been doing really good lately and even have a chance to make the playoffs this year.

About fifteen minutes ago she fell asleep, and Ken and Dad left the room. I'm alone with Mama. We have it planned so someone is always with her.

I'm leafing through Mama's Bible. I read two of the highlighted verses from Psalm 146: "Praise the Lord! Yes, really praise him! I will praise him as long as I live, yes, even with my dying breath." I look closely at the words, trying to make myself understand the words the way Mama does, trying to believe them. It's hard.

I read farther. "Don't look to men for help; their greatest leaders fail; for every man must die ... But happy is the man who has the God of Jacob as his helper."

I want to be happy. But how can I be when I know Mama's going to die?

"Kate." Her voice is so soft I can barely hear it, even though I'm sitting right next to her bed. "Dear Kate. I'm glad you're here."

"Dad and Ken are just in the other room," I say. "I'll get them."

"No, that's all right. They don't need to come in just yet. I had such a good sleep, such a nice dream."

"I'm glad, Mama." I squeeze her hand.

"I heard God's voice in my dream," she says. "He told me that no matter where I look in the Bible, he will speak to me. The verse will have some personal meaning, especially for me. Isn't that remarkable?"

"That's a great dream, all right."

"Can you get the Bible?" she asks.

"It's right here." I hold it up for her to see.

"Let's try it. Let's open it and point to a passage, like God says."

"Okay, Mama," I say.

I wonder if it will work. I hope I don't turn to a passage that lists a couple dozen "begats." I can't see that a list of who was born to whom would have much personal meaning.

I open the Bible.

"It's second Thessalonians," I say.

"Point to a verse," Mama says.

I close my eyes and put my finger on the middle of the page.

"Chapter three," I say. "Verse sixteen."

"Let me hear it," Mama says. "Let's see if there is truth in dreams."

I read, and I hope, for Mama's sake, there might be truth. I doubt it, but I hope anyway. I start to read out loud. "May our Lord Jesus Christ himself and God our Father, who has loved us and given us everlasting comfort and hope which we don't deserve, comfort your hearts with all comfort, and help you in every good thing you say and do."

"Yes," Mama says. "You see?" She closes her eyes. "God is good," she whispers.

I look at the words again. It's as if they are in big, bold black type. They almost jump off the page at me: **May our Lord Jesus Christ himself and God our Father, who has loved us and given us everlasting comfort and hope which we don't deserve, comfort your hearts with all comfort in every good thing you say and do.**

I hold the Bible to my breast. I wonder, was it just a dream Mama had, or did God actually speak to her?

Was it an accident my finger went to that verse,

or did God guide it?

All through Mama's illness I've been angry at God, and I haven't understood how Mama could be so calm.

My hands start to shake. They're shaking so bad I have to set the Bible down. "Mama, you've known all along," I say. I lean forward and kiss her cheek.

"Be comforted, my darling," she whispers. She squeezes my hand. I'm glad her eyes are closed so she can't see my tears.

twenty-seven

ginny's song

The church is packed. It seems like almost everybody from our church is here, and lots of other people, too. I'm sitting in the front pew. Ken is on my left, Dad on my right. I don't look back at anybody. I can't. Once the service starts, I keep my eyes closed. I have to. If I open them, the tears I'm holding inside might pour out in a flood.

We'd done a lot of talking to people at Mama's visitation, so when we got to the church we just walked right to the front. Well, not right away. I saw Allison. She didn't come over to me, but she looked at me and smiled. She nodded. I nodded back.

I got stopped by two people. Coach came over and gave me a hug. He didn't even have to say anything;

the hug said it all.

The only person who spoke to me was Mrs. Bennett, a lady from our church who I don't know all that well. She reached out and touched my hair. She held a strand of my hair in her hand and looked at it for a few seconds.

"You look so much like your mother," she said. "Such a wonderful lady." Then she dropped her hand and said, "Be strong."

I don't watch the pastor when he starts to talk about Mama. He tells how Mama's earthly pain has ended. Then he says words I've heard many times before. They take on a new meaning now. He says, "Now she's in the loving, comforting arms of Jesus." He talks like that's a good thing. I know the fact that her earthly pain has ended is a good thing. But I want her in my arms, not the arms of Jesus. I know I'm being selfish. I can't help it. Why should Jesus get to be with Mama, and not me?

I open my eyes after the pastor finishes talking. That's when Ginny goes up to sing. I asked her to. I told her that Mama would love to hear her sing one more time. It took me awhile to talk her into it, but she finally agreed. "I'll do it for your mama," she said.

I told her that one of Mama's favorite hymns was "On Christ, the Solid Rock I Stand," so that's the one she sings.

I sit there, listening. And thinking, "Listen, Mama. Isn't that beautiful? Ginny's singing just for you."

I close my eyes again, tight, because the tears are trying so hard to get out.

On our way to the cemetery I keep my eyes open. I don't care about the tears. There's only Dad and Ken and me and the driver of the car we're riding in.

At least it's a sunny day. It's the kind of day that Mama would have loved. I think how at least God gave Mama this one last sunny day.

I think about the last few days and wonder if this is how Ginny feels when she's on stage. I feel as if I've been on stage, first at the visitation, then at the funeral service, then at the cemetery. Everybody tries hard to say something that will make me feel better. I have to pretend it does.

Once we get back home after leaving Mama at the cemetery, I'm still not alone. Our house is full of people. Mrs. Loden from across the street arranged for people to bring food and to be with Ken and Dad and me. I guess they feel that we need people around us at this time.

I know they mean well. Everybody's been nice, they really have. Nothing can take the pain away, but it helps to know how much Mama was loved by everybody, not only me. At the visitation, we had a continuous slide show playing on the computer. Ken did most of the work on it, but all of us—Mama, Dad, Ken, and me went through hundreds of photos taken of Mama and of our family. We put together a little history of her life. Ginny helped choose the music that played in the background. The slide show was so beautiful, and so sad. Almost everybody who saw it had tears in their eyes. The same slide show is playing now in our crowded living room.

I stay in the house for a few minutes and try to eat some of the food. The tables and kitchen counters are filled with casseroles, desserts, and plates of sandwiches. I try to eat a little. But the first chance I get I sneak out to the back yard with some of the other kids who showed up.

We have enough for a little soccer game. Allison is here, and Ginny and Heather and Ivy and two other girls—one from my class at school and one from Sunday School. A couple of Ken's friends are here, too.

Nobody seems to worry about getting dirty. Dirt just doesn't seem important today. I think how if Mama were there she'd say something about how Ginny doesn't even seem worried that the soccer ball might give her a swollen lip. I think how if Mama were here she'd be right out here playing with us.

I hear the words, "Great shot, Allison!" And I'm surprised to realize I am the one who said them.

twenty-eight

the letter

For the first time since Mama's funeral, it is only the three of us in the house: Dad, Ken, and me.

Dad hands each of us a envelope. "Here's something your mother wanted you both to have. I haven't read either of them. All I know is that she wrote them especially for you."

"To My Kate"

is written on the outside of my envelope. I wait until I'm alone in my room before I open it. I take out the handwritten pages.

My dear Kate,

I had hoped you would never have to read this letter. I always held onto the thought that somehow it would be God's will that I live longer, that he would miraculously take the cancer from my body. I so much wanted to be with you as you grow beyond the beautiful young lady you are now, the young lady I am so proud of. I wanted to be right there to help you with the problems that you will surely face and to share in the joy of all your exciting discoveries.

But it's not to be.

God's will was for a different kind of miracle — the miracle of the life that you and Ken and your father have ahead of you, and of all the blessings you will share.

And yes, even the miracle of the lesson my illness has taught us all: that every day is to be cherished. That no matter how much time we have, or how little, we should use it as a time of love, of joy, of thanks. Earth is the right place for love (remember that poem by Robert Frost?).

But since it has been God's will that we all

begin a new chapter in the book that he has written for us, I am not sad. I am not even angry. I regret that we can no longer be together in body to share all the fun things that we so much enjoyed. I hope — I know — that you will remember our talks, our sports, our games, our camping trips, our quiet times. Even our Friday night popcorn.

We will always be together in spirit. Heaven is also the right place for love, and I rejoice that I will be with Jesus, just as Jesus will continue to be in your heart.

John Donne wrote a poem that said, "Death, be not proud, though some have called thee mighty and dreadful, for thou art not so... One short sleep past, we wake eternally, and Death shall be no more: Death, thou shalt die."

It's okay to cry, but do not cry long for me, for I am with Jesus, and I am free from the pain of my illness.

Do not cry for yourself, because you have a family and friends that love you, and you have the memory of our happy times together.

*Most of all, hold on to the knowledge
that I am with you in spirit, as Jesus is, and
you will never be without either of us.*

*My darling Kate, we have always shared
a special love. So turn quickly from your
mourning; the time for our love has not ended.*

It is still beginning.

With all my love,

forever and ever,

Mama

I start to read the letter a second time, but the
words are blurred. I wipe the tears from my face, but
still they keep coming.

I place the letter on my bed and go to the window. The moon is full, and I can see clearly the
flower bed Mama loved so much and worked in so
often. I can't stop the thoughts from rushing forth:
"Mama, please don't be angry with me for crying, I
miss you so much."

I close my eyes tight, just as tight as I can.

In the darkness behind my closed eyelids, I see

the bright outline of Mama's body—young and athletic and healthy. It will always stay that way. Always. And I see her beautiful face. I do! I see it so clearly it's almost like I can reach out and touch her cheek.

And the best thing of all—she isn't angry or sad. She is smiling.

I smile, too, and I walk outside. I have Mama's letter in one hand and my notebook in the other. I sit on the soft green grass next to Mama's flower bed. My legs are crossed beneath me, in the way I learned from Mama when we sat together so many times and just talked. I read her letter again.

My notebook feels like a close friend, someone I can share my secret thoughts with. I can't imagine a time when I'll ever stop writing my thoughts. I can't imagine a time when Mama won't be in those thoughts. She'll always live in my heart. I know that. My notebooks will always have something of her in them. By writing in my notebook I might be able to keep her alive even for those people who never got a chance to know her.

But right now, Mama, I'm just going to try to write a poem for you.

For only you.

I hope you like it.

never blame the umpire

For Mama

The loving arms of God reached out for you
And heaven has a brand new angel
Brand new lights to shine
So bright
Tonight.
Mama, who taught me about life
About love,
About the God I tried to push away,
I'm holding on now.
I'm holding on to the time we had
The silly times
The joyful times
The crying times.
And I'll remember
Just like you told me
To never
Ever
Blame an umpire.

Twenty Questions I'm Often Asked

1. Do you have a family?

I have a super family.

A terrific wife, Polly, who has put up with me during forty-five years of marriage. Wow! That's a long time! She's a nurse. When she worked in the hospital, her specialty was neo-natal intensive care. She loves working with babies. She also loves teaching others how to become good nurses. She just retired in 2009 after twenty years of teaching nursing at Tri-County Technical College in Pendleton, South Carolina.

Two wonderful and talented sons.

Tim is a history professor at Furman University in Greenville, South Carolina, and loves to play softball and baseball. He and his wife Jacquelyn have two daughters, Mireille and her younger sister Gabrielle. Don't get me started talking about my three wonderful granddaughters or I won't ever get to the next nineteen questions.

Andy is a realtor who lives near Lake Travis in Austin, Texas, with Kellie and their daughter Kaya and their two good-sized dogs, Arlo and Daphne. Andy loves all kinds of water activities. He also loves Austin, which is bad for Polly and me. If his family didn't love Austin so much we might be able to convince them to move closer to us so we could see them more often.

Luckily, both Tim and Andy can do many things they didn't learn how to do from their dad, like use computers and build things and fix things.

Two incredibly cute tiny dogs. Angel, a white toy poodle, and her brother Hunter, a black toy poodle.

2. What are your most favorite and least favorite chores?

Most favorite—mowing the lawn.
Least favorite—everything else.

3. I want to write and publish books someday. How can I get started?

First of all, read a lot. All the good writers I know are also people who love to read. Secondly, write a lot. To be a good musician or athlete, one must practice and practice some more. The same holds for writing: the more often you write, the better your writing will become.

4. When you're not writing, what else do you like to do for fun?

I love to play tennis and golf and softball and baseball. I play mostly outfield and shortstop on a softball team of "seniors" (that's a nice way of saying "old men"). We play more than seventy games a summer from March to October. If I were writing a scouting report about myself, it might say: "He hits for a high average, runs fast and is a good fielder, but he doesn't hit for power." I also play on an adult baseball team (for players 28 years old and older) with my son Tim. We play about twenty games a year. I pitch and play the outfield and first base. I love baseball. Can you tell?

I also love to collect and read three kinds of books: poetry books, young adult and children's novels, and sports books, mainly sports fiction. I have more than 7,000 books in my personal library, so I don't even have to leave my house when I feel like reading a good book, which I feel like doing every day.

5. How old were you when you started writing?

I don't recall ever writing a poem or short story until I got to college. I didn't start writing poetry (other than just a handful) until I was 33 years old. My first story and poems weren't published until I was 35. The problem is, even though I really liked my high school English teacher, neither he nor any of my other teachers in elementary or high school ever showed me how much fun writing a story or poem can be. Those of you who have teachers who encourage you to write poems and stories and show you how to get started are lucky.

6. Where did you grow up and go to school?

I grew up in Thomson, Illinois, a little town in the northwest part of Illinois, right on the Mississippi River. We had 500 people in town and eleven in my high school graduating class. I've written a lot of poems about growing up in Thomson. I went to college at Northern Illinois University in DeKalb, Illinois, and earned my Bachelor's and Master's Degrees there.

7. Are you rich?

I certainly am. But not in money. In satisfaction—the satisfaction of having great friends and a great family, and the satisfaction of waking up every day and looking forward to the fun things I can do and the new things I'll have a chance to write.

8. What's the hardest thing about being a writer?

For me, the hardest thing has nothing to do with the actual writing—it's trying to keep from getting too frustrated when a publisher doesn't want to publish something I think deserves to be published.

For some people, the hardest thing is coming up with

an idea and getting those first words on the page. That's not really a problem for me because I've discovered a lot of ways to help myself come up with ideas. I usually have more ideas than I have time to write them. But as a writer, I know how important it is to make time to write.

9. What's the best thing about being a writer?

Hearing someone who's read something I've written say, "Hey, I like it! It's not bad!" Getting published is a great feeling, of course, but that comes later, and that's just a bonus. There's great satisfaction in writing something, and great pride in knowing you've made it as good as you think you possibly can, even if it never gets published.

10. Do you have another job, or is writing the only work you do?

I taught school (English and creative writing) for twenty-eight years (one year of eighth grade—the rest in high school and college). Now I go around to schools and conduct some one-week poetry-writing residencies and do poetry writings and talk to students about writing and publishing. That's not work, though. That's fun.

11. How long does a poem have to be?

As long as you need it to be. Some say "As long as you want it to be," but I've found out that you might want a poem to be a certain length, but when you start to write it you find that it needs to be longer or shorter. My longest poem is 510 lines long. My shortest one is one line long. Its title is longer than the poem itself. Here it is:

The day I drew a girl as my opponent in my

first and only school wrestling match

She pinned me flat against the mat. And that was that.

I won't print my longest poem here. You'll need to find it someplace else.

12. Do you have any brothers or sisters?

Three sisters. No brothers. Janice was one year older than me. Because she was a year ahead of me in school, I always counted on her to "show me the ropes" and make things easier for me, and she always did. She died in December, 2004. Rita is 10 years younger than me and lives in Havana, Illinois. Rhonda, 12 years younger, lives in St. Charles, Missouri.

13. Sometimes I get frustrated because I don't understand a poem. It makes me not want to read poetry. What should I do?

Try not to think of a poem as a puzzle that has only one solution or one answer. Different readers will see something different in the same poem depending on their own experiences in life and their own experience reading poetry. Rather than ask, "What does the poem mean?" I think a much better question is, "What does this poem mean to you?" Or even, "What do you like most about the poem?" All you really need to do is try to enjoy something in the poem—the sounds or the story or the picture it paints or a surprising idea or surprising use of language. The meaning of a poem isn't as important as what it makes you think or how it makes you feel. You can enjoy it without "understanding" it in exactly the same way someone else might.

14. Do you draw the illustrations for any of your books?

Never. I'd love to be able to draw, but I'm as bad an artist as I am a singer. Luckily, when my books or poems require illustrations, the publisher finds someone else to illustrate them.

15. Which do you like writing best, rhymed or unrhymed poetry?

I love writing both. I think that anyone who wants to write poetry should practice writing both kinds. Some poems will work better if they rhyme, some if they don't. It often depends on the subject and the mood you want to create. It's important to give yourself the freedom to choose which approach works better. You can only do that if you practice writing in both rhyme and free verse.

16. What do you like writing most, poems or stories?

I like writing both stories and poems. One reason I started writing a lot more poetry when I was in my 30s and 40s was because I was busy preparing classes and grading papers as a teacher, and it didn't take me nearly as much time to write a poem's first draft as it did a story's. Most writing, of course, must be rewritten and revised many times. The best writers are those who discover that rewriting can be a fun experience and not something to be dreaded.

In recent years I've turned my attention more and more to the writing of full-length books.

17. Why do you write about baseball so much?

I've always loved baseball, ever since I was seven or eight years old and played by myself, throwing a ball against a wire fence in my back yard or tossing a ball in the air and then bunting it down a narrow sidewalk, trying to bunt it straight so it would roll a long way before going off into the grass. After playing on my first baseball team when I was thirteen, I've played on teams most of my life.

I've always been a big fan. When I was in school, I read all I could about the big leaguers and memorized all their batting averages. One of my favorite writing projects was to interview more than a hundred former major league baseball players for my books *Tales from Baseball's Golden Age* and *More Tales from Baseball's Golden Age*. These were players who were my idols when I was a kid. I never thought I'd actually have a chance to talk to them someday and listen to all their stories about their years in the big leagues.

18. What's your favorite baseball team?

In the American League, the New York Yankees.
In the National League, the Chicago Cubs.
It balances out because during much of my lifetime the Yankees almost always seemed to win their division and the Cubs almost always lost theirs.

19. Where do you live?

My wife and I both grew up in Illinois, but we've lived in Seneca, South Carolina, since 1991. We love living where it's warm most of the year.

20. What do you look like?

Some people think I'm a cross between Robert Redford and Tom Cruise. (Okay, so maybe I don't exactly LOOK like them.) But I'm old, like Redford, and I'm short, like Cruise.

Fehler, Gene,
  1940-

Never blame the
  umpire.